ODESSA ON THE DELAWARE

Introducing FBI Agent Marsha O'Shea

JOHN A HODA

The Old Man refused to die. The poker faces of the five powerful men surrounding his hospital bed gave nothing away, but Vladislav Balderis, his enforcer, knew what they were thinking. Who was going to take over now? The intravenous dripped a cocktail of drugs into the Old Man's veins to ward off further damage from the stroke he suffered overnight. The diagnostic machines whirled, beeped and chirped while the intubated ventilator pounded a steady beat forcing air into the Old Man's lungs.

Vlad put his debugging kit into his gym bag after scanning the room for camera lenses or listening devices. There were none.

Vlad found out the accountant had arrived at precisely 8 a.m. to the tidy row home on Cambria just off of C Street, juggling the Old Man's coffee and pastry with the *Philadelphia Daily Sun* and the *Wall Street Journal*. When he did not see him in the front parlor reading chair, he called out and heard no reply. Fearing the worst, the accountant rushed upstairs and found him lying face down on the bedroom floor naked. The Old Man was transported with a weak pulse and shallow breathing by ambulance to the tired Temple Episcopal Hospital.

The Old Man's lieutenants descended on the hospital at B Street and Lehigh Avenue from wherever they spent the night, with Vlad being the last to arrive. His 90-minute workout separated him from his cell phone tucked away with his MP-443 Grach pistol in his locker. Vlad understood why this man, wearing only a hospital gown, would not go easily. He heard many stories while driving for the accountant or the Old Man.

An old and cranky head nurse entered the room shaking her head. Her take-no-shit attitude shown through her readers perched on the bottom of her broad nose. There was more gray than black in her tight afro. She was a fireplug to be sure and took up a defiant stance. "If you are his family, why do you all have different last names?" she demanded.

"We are all his sons from different mothers," Arkady Valnikov said, looking up at her from across the Old Man's bed. He stood to his full height, a tad over six feet, the sweatsuit forming around his square bulk. Tussled short black hair and a day-old beard completed the picture of a middle-aged man who was rudely awakened.

"Only his family is allowed to see him while he on this floor," she replied turning on her heel.

The head of hospital security arrived in short order entering the brightly lit room with a purposeful stride. Older retired cop Vlad surmised from the Fraternal Order of Police ring on his right ring finger.

"What seems to be the problem here?" he demanded while turning down the walkie-talkie on his hip. The move was meant to open his blazer and reveal his shoulder holster.

"When did hospital square badges start carrying?" Vlad thought as he went back to busying himself with his cell phone while studying the ventilator set up that kept the Old Man alive.

"This is a unique situation we have here, Mr. Murphy," said Yury Yukolov, reading from the man's photo ID on a lanyard hanging from his neck onto his paunch. Yukolov turned and intercepted Murphy half-way between the doorway and the Old Man's Bed. Yury was the senior lieutenant in age and stature. He stood a full head above the shorter flabby ex-cop.

"He has no living family here in America," Yukushev followed. "He has raised us like sons in his business. We are his family and are deeply saddened by all this." He waved his hand at all the medical equipment dwarfing the Old Man.

Murphy said, "You realize that hospital policy requires me to inform you that his next of kin is to be the only visitors to ICU. Now when he is moved to a general hospital floor, you will—"

Arkady moved over to face the head of security at a closer than comfortable distance and said, "We were told that by the nurse, but as my brother has said, we are all that he has here. Certainly, an exception can be made, given the circumstances." Arkady reached out to offer a handshake.

The head of security awkwardly accepted the handshake and only registered slight surprise at the neatly folded $100 bills that he palmed and slipped into his pocket with a practiced nonchalance. He looked at all the three men towering over him. He glanced past them to the younger guy built like a light heavyweight who was busy with his smartphone. Murphy cleared his throat and said, "Yes, I understand now, given the circumstances. He would be alone without you. I will assure you all the privacy that you require during your visit. I'll tell the nurses now."

"Thank you," Arkady said.

Yukushev followed with, "Please visit us and help us celebrate when our father returns to health." With a simple a gesture of exchanging business cards, Yukushev handed the man passes to the VIP room of the Harbison Ave Sports Bar and Grille, a gentleman's club under the Old Man's control. Yury Yukolov patted him on the shoulder, and they gave the man some breathing room.

The other lieutenant that handled gas station skimmers, identity theft and insurance fraud nodded from the bedside in solemn agreement as the head of security backed out of the room. The accountant paid no attention to the drama and stood over his fallen comrade.

Each had a crew that handled different aspects of the Old Man's operation. Vladislav worked directly for the Old Man, as did the accountant.

Yury, the oldest man there and the most likely heir to the throne, spoke first. "The old goat thought he was never doing to die."

"Fools," Vlad interrupted, without looking up from the YouTube video he was watching on his iPhone and listening to from his Bluetooth earpiece. Under any other circumstance calling any of these men a fool, let alone all of them in front of each other, would be the end of Vlad, the enforcer.

Vlad paused the video and said, "You all acted as if this day would never come. You all thought he would live forever on a diet of Viagra, vodka and teenage whores."

An uneasy silence fell. Even though they were all old enough to be the hothead's uncle, only the Old Man was able to control Vlad. Where the others had autonomy over their operations and gladly forked over much of their profits to the Old Man, Vlad bristled at his lack of freedom to act on his own. His earnings from the electronics store and salary under the Old Man's hardened gaze were his only compensation. He was a resourceful tactician, but the Old Man constantly criticized him for not seeing the world strategically.

Vladislav Balderis stood there facing the older, softer men and decided that this time was going to be his time. Had he been instinctively waiting for this moment? Was it only the faint beating of the Old Man's cantankerous heart that was stopping him?

"You are respectable businessmen. You are held in high

esteem in your families and community. Some of you have done quite well for yourselves."

Pointing at Arkady, he continued, "Arkady, you have a mansion in the suburbs. You contribute to the church and many civic organizations. The Old Man built the waterfront operation that you profit from.

"Oh, Yury, tell me if it wasn't for the money laundering, how much could you sell the gentleman's clubs and sports bars for? Five million? Ten million? You have sent your children to prestigious schools, and now they are giving you grandchildren."

He looked at the others. "Which of you have used an ice pick lately, other than to prepare for a summer barbecue? Oh, that's right. That's Vlad's job. I hear what you say. Let 'Bad Vlad' handle that. Who does your 'wet work?' Those bikers at the clubs? Sure, they will break a few arms, but who makes people swim in the river never to surface again?"

Vlad was on a roll. "You don't have to do what I do. I make your operations run smoothly, I make your problems disappear, but today, I will be first to tell you that the rules of my engagement have changed. This thing of ours that the Old Man built is leaking profits. As you lead your comfortable lives, you don't care how much money is left on the table, do you? Do you ask yourselves why do we have to play nice with the other groups operating in this city? Do you ask why our terms are so lenient? What has happened to the Siberian Wolves? Who fears us in this city?"

Vlad wasn't finished yet. "Nobody rocks the boat; nobody makes waves. Keep it smooth. Stay under the radar, you were told. Everybody eats at the table. Everybody except for Vlad."

He looked at the Old Man now and addressed him bluntly. "As you got old, you forgot what made you who you were. You stopped taking risks. You let the others grab the money when it came to new opportunities. You would say to me, 'Vlad, this is a small fishbowl we swim in. We make friends with the bigger fish so we won't get eaten by them or have to eat their shit. Vlad, you are in a hurry, always in a hurry, slow down, let the money come to you.'" He paused. "I would bring you my ideas, and you would just shake your head and laugh."

Vlad placed his phone in his pocket walked over to the machine keeping the Old Man alive and applied the sequence he had just watched on the YouTube video, turned off the ventilator machine and cut off the signal to the nurse's station.

The Old Man shook violently, and his left hand shot out as his right arm was secured by the tape and tangled tubing that held the drip in place. As the Old Man shook and shuddered during an agonizing breath-deprived minute, the others were frozen and made no move to intervene.

Vlad grabbed the Old Man's hand in his and clenched hard. "Who is laughing now, Old Man?"

He held it until it went limp.

CHAPTER TWO

issed himself again. Cold and wet from his knees to his belly button, Sully staggered to his feet from the doorway of the Christian Science Reading Room alcove next to the steam grate. Sunlight didn't help his dehydration or searing hangover. Known as the Listerine Man by cops, EMTs, and business alike, Sully was known to chug mouthwash for its high alcohol content. Usually, people smell his sickly-sweet breath fifty feet away, but today, they get a whiff of his urine instead. At least I didn't shit myself, Sully thought.

Bodily functions aside, Joseph Sullivan was a mess, and he knew it. He destroyed his career and his family. He's been estranged for over two years from his wife and daughter. Sleeping outside on the ground has taken a toll on his shoulders, back, and feet. The reflection in the darkened storefronts was that of a straggly stringy-haired street bum wearing a tattered Phillies cap looking much older than a thirty-five year old.

He knew he was a far cry from the three-sport athlete at Bishop Egan High School and scout-sniper in the marines. That trim and scary strong warrior was invisible to passersby. He hated himself every time he asked them for spare change or a bite to eat. He was Listerine Man now.

As he made his way to the Unitarian church where a sympathetic janitor allowed him to store all his earthly possessions, he cleared a wide swath of unfortunate pedestrians who darted into stores or between parked cars to avoid him.

A flock of pigeons scattered on his approach, the flapping white and gray wings contrasting with their black shadows on the ground. In seconds, they soared in tight formation above him, impossible turns spiraling higher and higher, except for one. She was old and mottled. Her twists, which were slow and awkward, lost much of the altitude that she gained.

It was a blur out of the corner of his eye. In years past, he might have seen that threat as a cornerback blitzing from his blind side or an RPG whistling over his sniper hide. It nailed her in mid-turn and down to the ground they went. Peregrine falcons with their trim tails and short beaks are efficient Darwinists. Sully started sprinting. He had run in combat boots before, the chafing of his soaked underwear and sweatpants against his thighs was a reminder of Parris Island when he drove through swamps carrying his government issue M-16 and a full rucksack. Then was a time that he loved being alive. Muscle memory took him closer. The falcon had her in a death grip and was tearing away feathers and would soon get to the good stuff. It was close.

He lunged, and the falcon chose to fight another day, letting go just before Sully dove into the fray.

She was hurt and stunned, but not so much when she twisted out of Sully's saving grab. She nipped him on his arthritic knuckles. For good measure, she pooped in his hands before wriggling free. She gyrated helter-skelter into the nearby hedges.

No good deed goes unpunished, Sully thought, as he hoisted himself onto his feet under the glare of students who only saw the part where the injured bird escaped Listerine Man.

CHAPTER 3

What Ever Happened to Old-fashion Organized Crime?

By Stew Menke

How come you don't see mobsters doing the perp walk anymore? Every couple of years, the headlines would scream about the latest takedown of a crime ring. Five or six mugshots of sullen men with nicknames borrowed from gangster movies would be plastered across the top fold. On the page four-five spread, you'd see an organization chart of what family they belonged to along with bonus photos of locations of underworld activity and crime scenes.

Don't tell me the Pennsylvania Lottery and the casinos have taken away all the betting action around town. What, are there no chop-shops anymore? Are you telling me that the credit card companies have cornered the market on loan sharking? Is every fire at a furniture store or electronics shop in the middle of the night accidental nowadays?

Maybe it is me, but I can't remember seeing a French Connection bust at the Food Terminal or a TV news camera zooming into the trunk of a car pulled over on I-95 loaded with kilos of the white stuff.

What about that time when you were out on South Street grabbing two slices and a Coke after the game, and you saw a spotless Cadillac roll up and double park. Three guys in suits get out and stroll into the establishment. A few minutes later, they came out glancing around before sliding back into the Caddie. As the door with the tinted windows is closing, you see a wad of cash change hands to the guy in the back that never got out. No cop tickets their car as it blocked traffic and caused a lot of irate drivers. Before you knew it, they were off to their next stop. You're not dumb, deaf or blind. You weren't dreaming, but it's as if it didn't happen and nobody else seemed to notice.

Where have all the bad guys gone? Moved to Clearwater or sunny Arizona? Not likely, but I think I have a hunch.

Don't get me wrong; I'm not advocating a return to the days of drive-bys at the after-hours club or guys disappearing in the muck out by the airport. I'm just saying that coming back to the crime beat after forty years of writing about the simple game of baseball I noticed that the landscape changed. ICE black raid jackets, armored vehicles and SWAT teams seem to be capturing all the headlines and lead stories these days. Is that where all the Homeland Security money is going?

Back in the day, joint task forces were announced to combat organized crime, the never-ending war on drugs and anything else that would get good press and federal funding. These days, it's all about the threat of terrorism and the "illegals" inside our borders. The dubious connection is not lost on this former scrivener of sports.

Here is what I have concluded.

9-11 was the best thing that ever happened to the crime rings operating in this fair city and other major metros around the country. The Federales get a pass on their effectiveness on the war on terror. After all, how do you measure prevention? How do you measure deterrence? With all this attention, time, and resources allocated to the hyped-up threat of a terrorist attack, they can be justified in not prioritizing what had been the single most significant threat to society, pre 9-11. The city must use what meager resources it has for essential police services and chooses to continue to get tangled up with all the problems associated with putting their fingers in the dike of street-level drug dealing.

Then who is watching the racketeers? Sadly, it's not even the journalists. What happened to time-honored paper-selling muckraking? The tabloids are more interested in Hollywood breakups than gangsters breaking legs. Magazines? Fuggedaboutit. Cat videos on your Facebook feed get more eyeballs these days than subscription magazines.

Investigative journalism is all but dead, but thankfully for the good folks of Philly, I still have some gas in the tank, tread on the tires and just enough stubbornness to keep asking why.

The accountant kept returning to Stew Menke's column in the *Daily Sun* as he flipped between the local paper's business section and the *Wall Street Journal*. Menke came back to the crime beat after years of being the beat writer for the Philadelphia Phillies. His wit and voice continued to translate well to his loyal lunchbox readers, as he rediscovered his first love.

Sitting quietly in the Old Man's reading chair, staring out at the mid-January sleet and freezing rain, he drank the Old Man's coffee and ate the Old Man's pastry.

Now the Old Man was gone, the tidy house seemed so empty.

He couldn't even feel the Old Man's shadow. It happened too soon, that much was certain. Did he call the Old Man his friend? No, not really. Kindly employer? That didn't sound right either. Other than the ticking wall clock and pelting ice on the windows, the house was quiet. How long had he known the Old Man? The Odessa, fighting the Axis. The Old Man and the accountant had been through the wars, literally and figuratively, for seven decades together. Though tough and not always fair, he was still bluntly direct. You knew where you stood with him. They were comrades in arms. Somebody you were proud to fight alongside. Now he was gone. A part of him had died with Old Man.

He saw what "Bad Vlad" did at the hospital and how Yury and the others did nothing to stop the fucking kid. The accountant cursed them and himself, too, for their impotence. Why didn't we stand up for their helpless leader when he needed them the most? Were we afraid of that thug? Cowards all of us! he thought about himself as a younger man playing real-life hide and seek with the Germans and then the even harsher Soviets. That younger man would have fought Vlad to the death to protect his defenseless comrade.

The shock of what happened in the hospital suspended any conversation of an interim boss. Vladislav Balderis also made it clear that his work as an enforcer would now come at a hefty price. That had to be dealt with as well. There would be no protection payments holiday. The various government functionaries would still be expecting their bribes.

In a few minutes, he would go about his collections and payoffs with that hothead driving. What could he say to the brute? What would he say to him, if anything? You killed my comrade of over a half-century? No, he would keep his mouth shut, do his job and make a plan. That is what the Old Man was telling him to do, commanding him to be the avenging angel. He put down the newspapers, crushed the paper coffee cup, swept away his crumbs and stretched. The accountant now had a mission. After he went about his work that day, he would go to his apartment and put on his best black suit and shine his shoes. Then, he would go to the Old Man's wake.

The Old Man's connections went back over three decades. The accountant had kept meticulous records and updated them regularly. The favors given far outweighed the favors received. He expected many people of all ilks to be there tonight to pay their respects. His job was to get the word out that business would continue to go on as usual, until it was being decided who would succeed the Old Man. When it was over, and they were alone, he would ask the Old Man for counsel and not until then would he grieve. Oh, he would continue to mark the debits and credits; he was an accountant, after all, but he swore that he would make a plan. His thoughts returned to Menke, who was old school too. The Old Man would have probably not liked him, but he would have respected him. He glanced at the article one last time. With the passing of his employer, would old-fashioned organized crime return? Would it get crazy again? He tucked the newspaper into his briefcase with the ledger and cash. A chill ran down his spine as he locked the front door and scurried out to Vlad's armored-up black Chevy Suburban. He was troubled by the storm clouds of change swirling around this kid. He sensed an ill wind blowing into the Delaware Valley.

CHAPTER FOUR

"This is bullshit," Marsha railed to the newbie over her comm. "We've got the veritable who's who of Organized Crime out here tonight paying their respects, and it's only you, me and Ramit to cover it. Do you roger that Ramit?" she asked.

The intelligence analyst replied, "Yes, ma'am."

Marsha had plunked him in the back of a rented delivery van to watch the side door of the funeral home. He had the least essential eyeball so that he could enter the intel that she and the newbie were feeding him. He sat in a lawn chair with his laptop on his knees and Marsha's binoculars around his neck.

Marsha was quick with the retort, "Don't call me ma'am, Ramit, I'm not your mother."

"Yes, ma— Yesm Marsha," he replied.

It was Ramit who picked up chatter on the wires about the "Old Man" over the past couple of days. The bad guys were taking the night off to pay their respects to the Old Man. Fortunately, some agents did their homework on the Old Man a long time ago and their memoranda of interviews, or the slang term "302s," were still in the Bureau's servers. Who was this guy and why was every major player in this town paying their respects?

For years, it was assumed that the Russians were a loose confederation. Was this proof of a leader? Why wasn't there more intel on this guy? Marsha fumed.

Marsha guessed the Old Man dropped off the radar scope on the exact date when the FBI changed from federal law criminal investigations to a domestic intelligence agency that also conducted criminal investigations. That day was 9-11 when more American civilians died on one day from the coordinated terrorist attacks than all the servicemen and woman who died at Pearl Harbor, and still more died or are dying from breathing the carcinogens when they worked at the fallen towers.

In the good old days, she was a gunslinger in Miami with the Bank Robbery and Fugitive Squad. She also saw a lot of action on task forces with the DEA who worked a never-ending supply of narco cases. It was during this time that hubby Sean O'Shea gave her an ultimatum. Either quit playing cops and robbers and start making babies or else. Much to her mother's dismay, Marsha chose else. She decided to keep his last name, though.

When the squads were disbanded, and the Bureau became the Alpha dog of the twenty-two agencies that formed the Department of Homeland Security, Marsha decided to return home to Philly. She was now content to play out the string before retiring in nine years at 55.

She and the newbie sat on opposite corners of Renko's Funeral Home on Oxford Circle shooting video of every car's arrival. They put the footage in the encrypted FBI databases for Ramit to run the facial recognition software on of all the drivers and passengers.

On this bitterly cold night, the newbie had his hands full watching all the drivers and bodyguards who huddled together, talking, stamping their feet and smoking around their spotless idling black oversized SUVs to keep warm.

"There is a guy out here acting like he's the fuckin' Russian ambassador," the newbie said. "He's shaking hands, slapping shoulders and offering Dixie cups of something from a bottle. Do you have a make on him yet, Ramit?"

"Hold your horses," Masha said. "He's busy with all the people that are going in and coming out the front door. They are our priority right now. We get to the foot soldiers when it slows down."

"No sign of anything slowing down to me," the newbie groused.

Marsha had cajoled the newbie, Justin, fresh out of Quantico with an MBA from Stanford, to help out after hours and was now regretting it. Justin was getting his oxfords wet in the street work part of the job and didn't like it.

On the other hand, Ramit was never able to leave his bat cave as an intelligence analyst, and he was excited about doing some field work, even if he had a limited eyeball. The Special Operations Group that handled surveillance was otherwise occupied that night on a long-term assignment in Delaware County. She had to convince her supervisory special agent to approve the van rentals and to spring Ramit from the office. The handful of her remaining OC squad mates who had responsibility for the Sicilians and the drug cartels didn't think anything was coming from this intelligence surveillance and were home enjoying a warm meal with their families.

Wait until I put these photos up on their crime family's org charts tomorrow, she decided.

It wasn't quite the Appalachian meeting of 1957 of 100 mobsters in upstate New York, but it was good enough for Marsha. Here she was, woefully lacking resources, with all these clowns parading around like nobody was watching. They had some brass ones, that was for sure. After that meeting in '57, J. Edgar Hoover, the imperial FBI director, had to admit the existence of organized crime families operating on his turf. J. Edgar never wanted to tangle with the mob. He liked being a winner, and going up against the mob might make his vaunted Bureau look less than omnipotent.

Going on four hours now, she was getting great stuff. The link analysis from the intelligence gathered tonight would go a long way to prove that the underworld was alive and well. Now, maybe she'd get some respect for working the Non-Traditional OC groups.

Not to say that it was all Kumbaya out there. They came in separate waves. The Sicilians were first, followed by each other OC groups in some weird pecking order that she couldn't figure out. Lastly, the main Delaware Valley motorcycle gang wheeled in to end the night, followed by a stooped old man. Marsha had Ramit call all the gentlemen clubs in a twenty-mile radius, and each one was closed tonight for a "death in the family."

She couldn't risk another setup. Where they had been able to be part of the scenery outside the funeral home, arriving at the area around any of their clubs might cause suspicion. She, Ramit, and the newbie slowly disengaged to the predetermined vacant lot several blocks away. It would take weeks to make all photos into actionable intelligence, she thought as her personal phone buzzed. She looked at the text.

Delahanty's?

She replied: *Your turn to buy.*

After thanking both of her helpers that cold night, she cruised down Roosevelt Boulevard and made her way over to German-town Ave.

The text was code from her older brother Nick. Nick with the Philly PD Real Time Crime Center Unit or Fusion Center as some cities named them, who, like their father Nicholas Drummond Sr., was a captain. Drummond Sr. finished his career in vice.

Delahanty's is a blarney stone situated between their upbringing in Chestnut Hill and Center City in Manayunk. Last call was an amorphous time, usually when the barkeep decided to call it a night. The pitchers were cheap and the steam table stayed on for the best roast beef sandwiches in a town renowned for its cheesesteaks.

"…. And that is how it all went down tonight." Marsha downed the last of her mug, waggled the pitcher at her brother and said, "You're up big brother."

On his way back to the table in the back by the unused shuffleboard table with a fresh pitcher and two more roast beefs, he said to her, "That is a helluva story. I can pass it on to our OC Unit. They might have some loose threads that can tighten this up, but that's not why I wanted to get together with you before Sunday."

Since she had come back from the Sunshine State a decade earlier, she rejoined her family's Sunday evening dinners. Whether it was football or baseball season, dinner was held at the house at 6 p.m. Their mother did tolerate having the TV in the den loud enough if the Eagles or Phillies were still playing, but held the line on watching the game during mealtime. The Eagles were stunned in the playoffs this year, and it was still over a month before pitchers and catchers reported for spring training.

"What are we gonna buy Dad for his birthday?" he asked.

"He is so hard to buy for," Marsha replied.

"What about sending him and Mom to the Poconos for a 'Honeymoon Special?'" Marsha said, making air quotes.

Nick smiled and rolled his eyes. "You know Mom. She'll complain that we spent too much on them and that she never sleeps well in a strange bed."

"I guess that wasn't hereditary, huh, Nicky?"

"Look who talking, Marsha. Your thumb still sore from swiping on Tinder?"

It was a comfortable and relaxed banter between divorced and childless siblings.

"Seriously, Marsha, we can't buy him any more sweaters. Mom has me taking them to Goodwill with the tags still on them."

"Can't get him ball or show tickets. He can badge his way into any venue," Nick added.

Marsha thought for a minute. "Nick, when was it that Dad single-handedly disarmed the bank robbers?" That was just one of the Drummond stories that made their father a legend. It was passed around the holiday dinners like seconds on the mashed sweet potatoes.

"Christ, before I was born. Let's see. Maybe '66 or '67, why?"

"I was thinking of getting the headlines of the case off the microfilm at the library and framing it for his wall of fame in the den. Whaddya think?"

"You do it, and I'll pay for it," Nick said as both lefties toasted their success across the table in buying a birthday present for the man whom they adored but had everything.

They returned to finish their beers and beef and said goodbye in the parking lot.

Marsha could see that Nick was busy texting on his phone. She figured he was trying to hook up with a nurse coming off the 4-12 shift. Cops, firefighters, nurses, and food servers all needed to unwind after a long night. Nick already had a head start.

Vladislav Balderis was the subject line of the text she got from Ramit. It came with the newbie's close-ups of him drinking with the bodyguards in the parking lot of the funeral home. Ramit attached a copy of guy's current Illinois driver's license.

She looked over at Nicky's car to tell him, but he was already gone.

CHAPTER FIVE

He would be patient. The pick-up was going to happen. He had done his homework. He could be patient.

Born in Odessa on the Black Sea in Ukraine to a Russian naval officer and schoolteacher mother, he grew up in military housing. For a young boy, it was idyllic. He and his friends would play soccer in the courtyards until their mothers threatened to give their dinners to the dogs. They would roam in packs around the sandy beaches in the summer and play hockey on the frozen ponds throughout the city in the winter. Vlad learned English at the best schools, wrestled and played hockey to burn off his endless energy. He chose the army over academics and made his way through the GRU into the elite Spetsnaz with equal measures of aggressiveness and ruthlessness. It was in Georgia, during the ethnic cleansing of 2008, that his unit went too far. It was rumored but never proven that he took particular delight in the cruelties.

If not for political favors curried by his father, now a retired Deputy Chief of Naval Operations-Black Sea fleet, Vlad would have been exiled to the Manchurian border or worse. A man with Vlad's skills and temperament could be useful outside of Russia, and a deal was made for him to come and work for the Old Man. America was a playground, and with his rugged good looks, he had no problem finding playmates in the beginning. Not one for serious relationships, he scared off many of the women who didn't seem to appreciate his tastes. He was content to visit the Atlantic City casino rough trade call girls. Vlad saw America as a land of opportunity at every turn and wanted to be his own boss. Except there was one problem: How could he get around the Old Man? That was no longer an issue.

Vlad's special forces training made it possible for him to operate very effectively by himself. No team was needed now for what he waited to put into motion. Combining stealth, electronics and the willingness to kill up close made him the perfect choice to change the balance of power in this town. He smirked at the thought of how easy it would be. Hell, he and his teams had destabilized governments, neutralized threats to Russian sovereignty and committed all kinds of atrocities to strike fear in the local citizenry.

Finally, his quarry arrived. The nondescript van pulled up in front of the mid-block row house. Two men got out curbside and wasted no time punching the code on the keyless entry beneath the watchful eye of a panoramic camera. They were buzzed in. There wasn't a set up like this for ten square blocks of the squalor in surrounding North Philly. The driver of this plain vanilla van was lazy. He sat there smoking with his window down. All the effort to make the van bulletproof was negated by his stupidity. Vlad had watched this routine go on with little variation for weeks from a wireless camera he had planted in the area.

Moving in the shadows and away from any other cameras, Vlad crossed the street to the driver's blind side. He never saw Vlad until it was too late. Vlad's gloved left hand came out of his long overcoat pocket holding a .22 automatic with a homemade suppressor. Two quick taps to the head sent the man into the next world. Usually, Vlad would collect his brass, but this was part of the plan. Vlad grabbed the burning cigarette from the floor and extinguished it in the man's now slack and open mouth. He took the keys and pocketed them. Walking around the front of the van, he shielded his face from the camera lens, and when he was directly below it, he reached into his other pocket and pulled out an extending rod. Like he had done so many times before, he screwed on a tennis ball covered in petroleum jelly that he pulled from a baggie and extended the rod upwards to swab the camera lens with the goop. Those inside would not think twice about this camera malfunction.

He retreated to his secondary position. Breathing normally, he unsheathed his hunting rifle and waited. At least these Jamaicans had the sense to keep their drug house separate from the money house and in a few minutes he would have the daily take from their busiest North Philly territory. They should have moved this location but had gotten too comfortable, thanks to the Old Man's peacemaking. The idiots didn't bother to knock out the street lights illuminating the sidewalk between the row house and the van. He didn't even need night-vision for this turkey shoot.

The larger guy with his right hand in his coat pocket scanned the area for cops or passersby. He motioned to the shorter and stronger man carrying two satchels in both hands to come out. He held the rear passenger door open for Mr. Money Bags. He stood there motionless like he had done every time before. Predictable. His chest exploded from the high-powered round. The noise of the shot startled the other man, who dropped his bags and tried to dive into the van. Vlad led him with a headshot and one more into his torso. The man's momentum carried him only partially into the van's back door where he lay motionless.

Vlad collected his shells and walked to the sidewalk. Shooting both in the head with the .22 resulted in quiet, muffled reports, the only audible noise came from the brass tinkling on the pavement to be left there for the crime scene techs to photo, mark with numbered flags, bag and analyze. He gathered both satchels and walked two blocks to a rental with somebody else's license plate on it. He made sure to drive on busy streets in front of plenty of ATM cameras and closed-circuit TV security cameras. If the tints were not enough, he wore a wide-brimmed hat and wrap around glasses to hide his face.

He dialed up the feed for the gentleman's club. It was after hours. He could see in the faint light from the bar and dance floor. The next shot was of the exterior. Nobody was sitting in their cars getting something extra. The valet and regular parking areas were empty. It was the VIP room that he was most interested in. It was this room that was the ruin of many a good man as the song said. Footage from this feed would be shown to guys that had their pants down to the floor while their favorite dancer played into the blackmail scheme like they were doing a screen test for a porn shoot. It was here that Vlad acquired his next target for the night.

Leaving the rental running, he forced the side door of the club, knowing that the silent alarm would trigger only at the Old Man's house.

We will deal with any fool stupid enough to break into our place better than the cops, the Old Man said.

Vlad made his way to the VIP room. There was no music playing. No thump of bass penetrating thin walls. On the couch, where he usually sat for these occasions, was Yury Yukolov, the Old Man's logical heir apparent. His head lolled back and forth back in ecstasy. His favorite dancer was between his splayed legs with her head busy in his crotch. Vlad came in, unseen by both of them. He closed the distance between the door and his prey like a striking cobra. His focus on the action and the darkness of the room didn't allow him to see her mardi-gras beads on the floor. He skated to an abrupt stop, bumping her kneeling frame forward.

Vlad's aim was thrown off as he tried to bring his weapon to hit center mass.

Instead, he angled his first shot through the back of her head into Yury's penis. Yury's eyes opened in shock. He jerked backward and stood up straight up. The dead dancer dropped to the carpeted floor in a heap. Looking straight into Vlad's eyes, through the pain and with the surprise of the ambush wearing off, he realized what was coming next.

"Not in the face, Vlad."

"Too late, Yury," Vlad replied.

Vlad checked his watch that he had set on a timer. Less than 78 seconds in and out and that included breaking into the security office to destroy the camera feed and its memory card. His left knee began to throb from his near fall into their sex. Was he more upset with his carelessness or that he might find his face in Yury's lap as well?

Did he stop somewhere for ice or keep to his schedule? He cursed himself again for not shielding his face while driving a preselected route to his last stop past ATMs and businesses with outward facing security cameras.

The row houses on Eighth near Oregon in South Philly were perfectly manicured. The street parking was unofficially predetermined, and even on game day at the nearby ballparks, no one dared take an empty spot.

The sidewalks were clean enough to eat from. He pulled his collar up to his ears to ward off the cold in the frigid pre-dawn hours. Vlad strolled along till he found the car that he was looking for. It was the exact match to his rental. He bent down and took the loosely-affixed rental license plates from the vehicle and reattached the correct plates to it that he had used on the rental. With a fob that matched the electronic signals exactly, he popped the trunk and deposited the van's keys, money satchels and the .22., and quickly closed it, but not before ripping out the wires to the brake lights.

He retraced his steps to the rental, put on the rental's plates and drove through surface streets back to the rental agency where the crews laundered their cash. He retrieved his Suburban. He listened to his favorite entrepreneur podcast as he made his way to his Society Hill condo with two brief stops. First to the waterfront to toss the rifle. The overcoat, gloves, hat, glasses, and shirts were next shoved into a trash compactor. He put on his gym clothes. Before arriving at his Society Hill condo, he made the text from his burner phone, got the confirmation back and tossed it down a sewer.

In a few hours, he'd be rolling on the mat with some meathead at the martial arts studio. Maybe he'd have the pleasure choking out a newbie cop who joined with the "police discount." Business as usual until he was ready to make his next move.

CHAPTER SIX

Sully didn't want to show up stinking drunk. That was his rule. He wasn't about to disappoint the one guy who talked to him like a human being. Why Stew took an interest in him was a mystery, but over the fall and early winter, they would meet at the soup kitchen on Tuesday nights and talk. As Sully washed his hands and put on the hairnet, he thought about the time that he rode back to Stew's apartment in shouting distance of the Temple University campus and they would talk about their experiences in combat.

Stew would point to his prized 35 mm camera on the fireplace mantle and bring out the photo albums. Stew had been an AP stringer in Vietnam. Itching to see combat, he got on a copter with replacements headed into the central highlands combat base of Khe Sanh, just before all hell broke loose. He stayed as two marine regiments held the fort against two well-trained NVA divisions.

Sully talked about two tours in Afghanistan as a marine scout sniper.

Back in the late '60s and '70s, they didn't have a clue about PTSD. Stew could talk to Sully about how returning vets came back home, scorned by their age group as baby killers. They suffered alone with their struggles. They could only talk with other vets at the American Legions or VFWs about the horrors of war.

Sully began to realize how his return to the world was very similar. Sully came home and got a job doing logistics planning for a freight company. He married his high school sweetheart and shortly after that had a baby girl. Everything seemed normal.

Okay, he admitted to himself, he overreacted to loud noises and didn't like being in large crowds, but otherwise, he was functional. Hunting in the Bucks County farmlands for small game and in the Poconos for whitetail deer lost its appeal when he started seeing the faces of some of the Afghani kids who were planting IEDs in his rifle scope.

Sure, he acknowledged that he drank more than in high school or when he wasn't in the sandbox, but he shook it off as part of the adjustment to civilian life. He told himself that he drank so that he wouldn't have the nightmares. What he couldn't deal with was that everything that was bottled up in that squared away marine began leaking out.

Slowly and gradually, the drinking binges happened more often and more heavily. The more he tried to quit, the worse it seemed to get. His wife became alarmed at the lost weekends, and he promised to cut back. He'd be good for a while, and then he'd find himself waking up from a blackout. Then he started abusing her. She couldn't live with his Dr. Jekyll and Mr. Hyde personalities; the cops came, she got a restraining order and told him to get out.

Stew was dishing beef stew from large trays, and it was Sully's job to keep the trays full. Vets that were drunk, high, or off their meds and were acting out could not assist. Yes, Sully was dying for a drink. He tried to hide his shaking hands by keeping them busy.

The soup kitchen was the brainchild of Ellis Long, iconic first basemen for the Phillies. Temple University donated the food and fundraisers purchased the surplus from mobile kitchens which were entirely staffed by the vets. City-owned abandoned building lots like the one here on Frankford Avenue in Kensington became the meeting places. Other city, state, non-profits and religious groups provided much-needed resources in clusters of tents that were set up an hour before serving time. Third-year law students worked with Legal Aid to help the working poor and homeless cut bureaucratic red tape. A health triage unit staffed by ER docs, nurses and EMTs did their best to treat and refer. Church vans stood by to transport the increasing numbers of homeless to church basements that became overflow shelters when sub-freezing nights were on the forecast. It worked and became a model for other cities to follow.

"I'm getting low here, Sully."

"You got it, Stew, the cook said the next batch is almost ready."

Sully grabbed the empty pot and hustled back to the cook who tasted the batch and proclaimed it ready. In his hurry to grab the pot and get back to the line, the gravy sloshed out of the pot onto his bare hands. The pain was excruciating. Drop it or get it ten more feet to Stew. He collided with Stew as he dropped the pot onto the serving station and some of the contents spilled out onto Stew's arm, burning him.

"Damn it, Sully, be more careful," Stew said, immediately regretting it when he saw the burns on Sully's hands.

"Are you okay, Sully?"

Through his tears and the searing pain in his palms and fingers, he replied, "I'm good."

Stew turned to Sully and said, "Go over to the first-aid tent. I can get somebody else to run for me."

Torn between duty and the throbbing pain, Sully said, "I'll be right back."

He zig-zagged his way over to the first-aid tent and waited patiently for the triage nurse. When it was his turn, he just held out his hands.

Her eyes widened at the sight of reddening skin and blistering on the back of both hands. She quick-stepped him over to the porta-sink and put his hands under the lukewarm water. Patting them dry, she applied the salve and wrapped his hands from fingertips to wrist. The salve and lack of air on them reduced the pain, but he knew he would be in for a miserable night.

All the food prep guys and servers were now seated at empty tables.

"Over here, Sully." Stew motioned him to an empty seat next to him with a full bowl covered by waxed paper and a large piece of cornbread in front of it.

Sully nodded and sat down grabbing the cornbread first. It was his favorite. Through the pain, he still managed to say, "If God made anything better, he kept it Heaven."

Stew had made quick work of his meal and was having his after-dinner cigarette. There was nobody to tell him to put it out in this crowd. "So do you think the Phillies got a chance this year?"

Sully swallowed and replied, "What, to break .500?" Stew was the only one ever to ask his opinion on anything. "How many one-run games did they lose last year?"

"Twenty-nine. Most in baseball. They won only fifteen of them," Stew said. Just because he didn't fly around the country watching them play for several years now, didn't mean he didn't keep track.

"No decent closers, no setup guys, no middle relievers. They all took turns screwing the pooch last year," Sully replied.

"Yeah, the bullpen was so bad they should have put a subway

turnstile on the bullpen door with the number of guys that were in an out of there," Stew said.

This was the acerbic wit that Sully remembered reading from the time he was old enough to tie his shoes until Stew's last feature column. "So what's this I hear that you are taking on the mob, Stew? It's not like we're talking about the New York Mets here," Sully said.

Stew said, "Yeah, be careful what you ask for. No sooner I opened my mouth, bodies start dropping everywhere." He looked around and made sure nobody was eavesdropping. "Word has it that the guys from South Philly were responsible."

Sully asked, "How's that?"

"My sources tell me that the cops were tipped off and as soon as the goon got out onto Broad Street, they pulled him over for a tail light violation. It's on their dash camera where they got his consent to search the car. He was bragging that he had nothing to hide and told them to go ahead, knock themselves out. When they pulled out the money bags and a .22 with a suppressor still attached to it, he went batshit crazy as they tried to cuff him, screaming he never saw that stuff before in his life."

Sully was still shaking his head as they got up and made their way to Stew's beat up '66 Mustang. They talked more about what that could mean and how it might incite a mob war.

They were coming up on Stew's apartment a block away, and Sully looked out his side window into the dark, cold and saw three college kids loitering across the street from a State Store. He asked Stew to drop him off at the corner, pretending that he needed to tend to the throbbing in his hands at the pharmacy where he usually bought the Listerine.

"Take care, Sully, get back home safe, you hear," Stew said as Sully closed the door.

Sully got back to the college kids, who were obviously under-age. He knew the drill. They would give him cash, and he would go into the State Store and buy them liquor. He could keep the change or buy himself something that would go down smooth. He reasoned that it would help with the pain in his hands. Not that he needed a reason.

Stew parked near his apartment and limped to the front door. Because one leg was shorter than the other, he couldn't play competitive sports and was rejected by the draft board. He shuffled a bag of soup kitchen leftovers that he was carrying to fetch his front door key from his Phillies warm-up jacket.

"Excuse me, Mr. Menke. May I have a word with you? I know something about the murder at the Harbison Avenue Sports Bar and Grille the other night."

Stew turned around to see a slightly older man who had just spoken to him with a Russian accent. The man wore a fedora over a long dress coat, a plain suit coat, white shirt and tie clinched up to the top button and glasses. He was holding a copy of the organized crime article written by Stew. "Sure. C'mon in. Don't mind the mess."

The accountant smiled and said. "Thank you for receiving me unannounced at this time of night."

CHAPTER SEVEN

"Until a few days ago, I worked for Vasily Pavlichenko. He died in the hospital from a stroke. I know that his life, no matter how close to death he was, ended at the hands of the man who murdered someone at the gentleman's club."

Stew was confused. He didn't know anything about this Vasily fellow. "Please tell me more about Vasily."

"Your paper ran a small obituary of him. He was listed as having no family and was a retired exporter, but here is the real story." The accountant began:

"Eleven-year-old Vasily Pavlichenko became orphaned at the beginning of World War II. It was during the siege of Odessa that his parents were killed. He scrambled to stay alive during the siege and subsequent Axis massacre and occupation. By night, Vasily was a runner for black marketeers, and by day, a messenger for the partisans hunkered down in the city's catacombs. His life as a teenager, under brutal Soviet rule following the Red Army's retaking of the town, was much worse. Many Ukrainians chaffed under the iron fist of Stalin's *apparatchik*. He became a soldier in the black market gangs at the U.S.S.R.'s busiest port. This was when I met him."

The accountant stopped and looked around the room for the first time.

Stew said, "I can put a kettle on. Tea or coffee?"

The accountant relaxed back into the second-hand armchair and replied, "Tea, if it's not too much of a bother."

Stew hustled to the kitchen and started the water and rubbed two mismatched cups clean with his dishrag and returned to see his guest puzzling over his collection of memorabilia.

"I was a sportswriter for many years before I returned to the crime beat," he said waving to the baseball shrine in his living room. "Please continue."

With renewed focus, the accountant complied. "Vasily rose in the ranks, but not without many skirmishes with death and untold hardships in prison. Let me tell you, Mr. Menke, many men become hardened in prison. Vasily became smarter. It was during those dark days of the Cold War that he learned how to enrich our crew working the waterfront while lining the pockets of naval officers, who looked the other way when high-end western consumer goods came to port, hidden in the leaky freighters. One particular young officer, Leonid Balderis, was especially pliable with cash and women. It was this man that called in the favor with the Old Man years later."

The tea kettle whistled, and Stew stood up again. "Would you like it with milk or sugar?"

"Both."

Stew arrived with two cups in saucers, tea bags floating in both.

"Thank you." The accountant bobbed his tea bag and finally took a sip and nodded.

"The Old Man?" asked Stew wondering where this conversation was headed.

"I am sorry, forgive me. To us in the business, he was the Old

Man, to the rest of the world he was just an old man, an unassumingly quiet old man."

"How did he come to America?" Stew asked.

"The Old Man was neither Russian, nor Jewish, but with forged papers, he was able to enter into the 1980's mass emigration of Russian Jews from Odessa to the United States. Many of the Russian Jews ended up in the Brighton Beach section of Brooklyn at about the time that Vladislav Balderis, the son of Leonid Balderis, was born. I will get to Vladislav 'Bad Vlad' in a minute."

The accountant set the teacup down on the stained coffee table with too many markings from cigarettes that tipped out of the decorative ashtrays and continued. "The Old Man's good work in Brooklyn first started with protection rackets. God forbid that a jeweler or electronics dealer miss a payment. He'd take an eye for an installment on the next payment. That and many other talents awarded him a fresh start with a franchise in Philadelphia."

Stew saw where this was going and let the man continue, urging him forward with his full attention.

"When the Soviet Union collapsed, he called out to me to come here and handle his books for him. When I arrived, he told me his secret."

Both men now leaned forward over the coffee table, their cups and saucers placed like pawns on the chess

The accountant continued, "The Old Man offered a disarmingly simple proposition to the leaders of each crime group. He could help them keep and grow what was theirs. Over time, he smoothed out the rough spots on territorial disputes. Agreements were forged that nobody would take a slice of another man's pie, and if they did, the Old Man was vigilant in squashing any upstart organizations from muscling in on anybody's action. He quietly began to prove to these hardened men that they made more money expanding their businesses without having to take from their neighbors."

Stew wasn't comprehending this. "One second. How did he make money on this?"

"The Old Man built his crew from freight terminals along the waterfront on the Delaware River where stolen goods such as high-end automobiles went out, and Eastern European women desperate for a fresh start came back in some of the same cargo containers. He helped get rid of the low-rent titty bars and moved the girls into high-end gentleman's clubs that he controlled.

"For a surcharge, he facilitated payments between the various organized crime groups and those sworn to stamp out crime and corruption. He was a perfect cut out. City hall didn't want to approve the redevelopment project? Licensing inspectors or building inspectors shutting down your operations? Not a problem. His 'gentlemen's clubs' were high end, spotless and perfect for blackmailing civil servants and politicians and all this went under the radar for years."

Stew brought out some sugar cookies on a plate to share. The accountant picked out a broken one, took two bites of it and sipped his tea.

"From there, Vasily masterminded the three I's: Insurance Fraud, Influence, and Identity Theft. As he grew each enterprise, he awarded the franchises to his highest earners."

Stew listened and munched on his cookie. He was torn between being a good listener to this man eulogizing his dead friend and wanting to reach for his reporter's notebook.

"Vasily stayed away from drugs and stuck to white collar crime which had the advantages of high payoffs and low detection with only a slight risk of time in the Federal country club prison system. He compared that soft time to life imprisonment or a painful death that he escaped from the Gulags."

"Why don't I know anything about this man?" Stew asked.

"He never brought attention to himself. Understand, he never lost sight of his true calling as a middleman." The accountant took the other portion of the broken cookie to balance his take from the plate.

Stew took this all in. Maybe it wasn't all about the good guys just wanting to search out terrorist post-9-11. Maybe some detente was reached with the rival gangs and they all started flying below the radar. "What about this Bad Vlad character?"

"The Old Man employed former KGB on a contract basis but agreed to bring a hot-headed and disgraced Special Forces operative to America to do his real dirty work. Sure, the Old Man used the local motorcycle gang as his ad hoc bouncers and enforcers at the clubs, but it fell upon Vladislav, Leonid's son, to do the wet work, things that couldn't be trusted to anyone else. It was this trust that eventually killed him."

"How so?" Stew asked.

The accountant asked to use the bathroom. Stew knew this information was going to be front page news when he broke the story. He listened to the toilet flush, and the sink faucets turn on and off. Upon his return, he saw that the accountant had run the towel across his face. His eyes were still wet from wiped away tears.

He began slowly and looked straight down into his empty teacup. "I found the Old Man at home, having suffered a massive stroke. He was barely alive when he arrived at the hospital. His lieutenants then assembled there. The hospital stabilized him, but there was no hope for recovery. The men that he made rich were standing around with their thumbs up their asses. What were we to do next? The Old Man made no plans for succession. We all thought that he would live forever, you know."

He paused and stared at the five decades of autographed photos and signed baseballs above Stew's mantelpiece of baseball players.

Stew waited.

"The kid decided to take matters into his own hands, and to a man, we all did nothing to stop him." With that, this humble accountant opened his satchel and took out his Chromebook and inserted a thumb drive. "The Old Man had a separate camera feed than that of the security cameras in the club that he could watch from his home. This camera feed didn't go through the security system. It also came with sound. He used to tell me it was free porn. If he liked a girl that he saw, he would ask me to bring her over. The girl would be given a wad of cash and told to say nothing about her visit."

Stew watched the HD picture come alive with a man sitting on a couch moaning in pleasure. The ceiling camera was placed at the angle to catch the action from behind the sofa. It captured the seated gentleman and a naked girl's head bobbing up and down in his lap.

"That is Yury Yukolov, the man who most likely would have succeeded Vasily," the accountant narrated.

Then Stew saw a shadow coming into the frame from behind the girl. It became a hand with a gun. The gun had a silencer on it. The hand became an arm, and then a man lurched forward into the scene. A clear facial view of the man was seen as he clumsily squeezed a round off into her head. The noise was startling, but not as startling as the shrill hiss from the man on the couch who catapulted into a standing position as the girl fell off his lap onto the floor.

Stew could make out the man say "Not in the face, Vlad," and the reply from the gunman, "Too late, Yury." The next two shots blew the man's brains out. The gunman disappeared from the frame.

Stew stared stone-faced at the monitor. "He just killed those two people like it was nothing."

The accountant let the video play on of the two dead bodies

with their blood spooling out onto the floor. "He must be stopped. It is not too late to put the genie back in the bottle."

"Why me and not the authorities?" Stew asked, fixated on the computer screen.

"I know too much. I was too close to the Old Man. I am afraid that I am on a short list of names that Vlad wants to cross off. I have begun arrangements to leave the country. I am alone, I have no family, and I want nothing to do with the authorities' promises or their witness protection program. If Vlad kills me before I can flee, my comrade's death would never be avenged. Hold onto to this until you know that I am far, far away or that I am dead."

"How will you reach me?" Stew asked.

The accountant stopped the video feed and ejected the thumb drive and handed it to Stew. He then toggled over to a book-marked website and there in the comments section was a post from Sparrow. He pointed to a number in the post and said, "It's the daily lottery number. If you don't see a post from Sparrow with that day's number, then you know I'm dead, or I have made it to where nobody can find me."

CHAPTER EIGHT

Vlad and the remaining Russian capos, Genrikh Yukushev, Arkady Valnikov, and Leonid Chernyshevski stared at the closed coffin of Yury.

"The Sicilians will pay for this," Vlad said.

"Why would they do such a thing? What is their end game?" Arkady asked.

"They saw the power vacuum the Old Man left and wanted to destabilize our organization. Don't be surprised if they try to take over the gentlemen's clubs and sports bars. They get the cash cows and can take over blackmail and extortion at the same time," Vlad warned.

"I'm not so sure of that," Arkady replied.

"They were so brazen in the attacks. They didn't bother to throw away the evidence or use a stolen car," Vlad replied testily in a less than respectful tone in front of the dead.

"Exactly my point. When did you know any group, except gangbangers, to be that sloppy?" Arkady left that question to hang in the flower-scented air as the soft funeral home music droned on.

Yukushev and Leonid stood silently as Vlad and Arkady spoke their differences.

"We must get stronger and protect what is ours. I have army comrades back home tired of running around Ukraine. We can arrange school visas for them, and they will be your bodyguards, and I will use them when we strike back and believe me, we will avenge poor Yury," Vlad said.

They all returned to looking at the casket. A framed photo of its occupant from his younger days stared back at them with a dark stare mocking all of the middle-aged men standing there, Vlad thought it would be time soon to allow Yury's blood relatives murmuring in the adjacent room to grieve the loss of their loved one.

Vlad didn't think that the consolidation of power would be this easy. These men thought of themselves as independent businessmen, just with the minor point that most of their earnings came from illegal businesses. White collar crime was lucrative, but made these men soft, Vlad realized.

He was not just content to skim a more significant portion of their take for their protection. He had bigger plans of playing the other OC groups against each other, weakening them. The groups would inevitably start fighting. He and his cadre of enforcers would strike when the timing was right.

Leaving Renko's Funeral Home late afternoon after all the mourners departed, Vlad took special care to park his Suburban and wait in the shadows for the right time to steal the car he needed for this night's special operation. He moved quickly and efficiently in taking the car. He moved all his equipment into its back seat and adjusted the seat and the radio dial.

The GPS signal from the Sicilian consigliere's car still showed it parked outside of their social club on Passyunk near Tasker. He had placed the GPS there while backslapping the car's driver and feeding him shots of vodka at the Old Man's wake.

Just inside the top of the front wheel well wasn't the best place for a GPS unit with all the salt and slush on the highways this late in January, but it still transmitted a clear signal. Vlad thought about the times that he sat next to Old Man with the consigliere. He was the voice of reason when the hotheads on his side of the table talked of violence and death.

Vlad was idling on Torresdale Avenue across from the Dominican's club. Warren Marichal and Robbie Mondesi were at their usual booth with their entourage. He watched them enter an hour earlier. They brought fentanyl to the city with devastating consequences to the Frankford section. Taking them out in a crowded bar wouldn't work for many reasons. He made it simple by duct taping the crude IED under their table when he broke into the club on the previous Monday night when the club was closed. He didn't need line of sight for his radio-controlled transmitter. He was just waiting for the women to go to the bathroom before he detonated it. He could see them thanks to the high-def pinhole camera he installed across the floor from their raised VIP table and it was transmitting a festive scene.

The DJ had people up dancing in the lighting that pulsed with the music. The bottle girls were doing a brisk business. The small charge he attached to the camera came from a Cuban grenade, and it would obliterate the camera when he detonated the IED. Keeping with the old school tradition of not killing innocents would point this attack to their competitors. Using the same crude parts, he had fashioned the IED that was sitting behind him in a gray plastic storage tub. This would connect the Dominican's competitors to the next killing.

Vlad sat waiting for Champagne, the promise of nose candy and a weak bladder to make for the perfect storm. He felt comfortable sitting in this stolen car with legit plates, as the owner hadn't reported it stolen yet. He'd return it at the end of the night in the competitor's turf just around the block from where his

Suburban sat. So simple. Get everybody pointing their fingers at everybody except the Russians and let nature take its course.

The girls tried dragging Marichal and Mondesi to the dance floor, and the men shrugged them off. The girls left their purses there and hustled out on impossibly high heels to dance to their latest fave. The DJ followed with another song that kept the girls grooving to the beat. He finished the set with a slower song, and with no men to grab onto, they walked back to the table, finished their flutes and grabbed their Gucci handbags with all sorts of goodies in them.

Each kissed their man and Vlad would see to it that these kisses were to be the drug wholesalers' last. He controlled their fates now. He imagined the girls weeping and wailing at the funerals. When the girls cleared the room, and the dance floor was empty between sets, Vlad pressed the button. A muffled whoop came from the building as several windows shattered from the concussion. The shaped charges concentrated the shrapnel directly toward the seats and away from the dance floor. The screaming started as acrid black smoke rushed out the front door past the toppled bouncers. Sensitive car alarms added to the cacophony. Once-festive partiers now rushed bloody and stumbling from the smoke and noise out into the street. It was bedlam, and Vlad slowly cruised away in the car with its tinted windows.

The lights on Broad Street were timed perfectly for his slow-motion getaway. He snaked around city hall and then ran along Market to Sixth Street towards his next stop. He always gazed at the buildings that housed the FBI and the U.S. Attorneys for the Eastern District of Pennsylvania as he drove past. He was happy to never set foot in either building. His music was soft jazz, and he tapped his gloved fingers to the sax solos.

It wouldn't take long for the news to circulate of the bombing. The consigliere would rush to meet his boss to discuss this. Was it a terrorist act? Was it payback for past sins? The boss wouldn't leave his house. They would come to him, and that was in the direction the consigliere car was pointed. His driver would let him in the car, and he would be riding in the rear on the right side, the same as when he arrived at the Old Man's wake. The car was expensive but was not reinforced or bulletproof. Vlad had made sure of that when he spent time with its driver that night. They ran out of the building.

They jumped into the car and fired it up. Vlad's GPS tracker showed they left the club and began speeding as expected toward his position. He pulled from a parked position a half block away from the tourist trap cheesesteak places and dropped his package below his car and waited for them to stop behind him mid-block. They couldn't get around him on this tight city street with parking on both sides. The driver was very impatient and beeped his horn at Vlad to move.

Slowly, Vlad moved forward, and the consigliere's car occupied the space where Vlad's tardy car had sat. The driver was too pissed to care about the brown Acme grocery bag laying on its side that was now directly below the seat of his precious passenger. Vlad stopped again. The driver beeped again, this time more impatiently. Vlad gunned his engine while detonating the device in the bag. The consigliere's car rose several feet in the air in the blast. The armor piercing titanium shredded the unprotected undercarriage followed by the white phosphorus that lit up the interior of the car like a gigantic flashbulb. The shock pushed Vlad's car forward like a toy.

He whistled a jaunty tune from his prep school days back in Odessa. He knew what havoc bombs would make going off in the city. It wouldn't take the authorities long to dismiss terrorist acts given that the same explosive charges were used and the targets were organized crime members. The government had to assure the populace that only bad guys were targeted.

Vlad dragged the dead body of his car's original driver from the trunk and placed him in the driver's seat. The same type of bomb was placed on the seat next to him. Vlad made the explosion only a half charge. The bomb technicians would conclude that the device went off prematurely and the investigators would determine that this soldier of the Columbian cartel died in the battle raging to control Philadelphia's drug trade.

Vlad was feeling elated with his plan's execution. His skills and technical know-how were paying off. He felt his new burner phone vibrate. He looked at his screen.

Have to meet ASAP!

Vlad texted back, *Can't. Busy.*

How soon can you get there? The source persisted.

This source is not running me, I'm running him. Vlad pushed back with. *It can wait.*

Have it your way. The club had a separate camera feed with sound apart from the security system.

CHAPTER NINE

"Your brother tells me you got money shots the other night," he said.

"Who knew Vasily Pavlichenko was a player," Marsha replied.

"We only knew him as the 'Old Man.' Don't feel bad, he was a ghost to us too."

"What I can't help wondering is that his body was not even in the ground and other bodies start dropping like dominos," Marsha added.

Her brother Nick had reached out to Detective Sergeant Mike Hollins in the Organized Crime Unit. In the spirit of inter-agency cooperation, Marsha decided to eschew her task force contacts and speak directly, so there was no miscommunication or filtering. Now they started the game of each side flipping their cards over one at a time.

"Listen, Agent O'Shea—"

"Marsha, please," she interrupted.

"All right, Marsha. I'm getting a lot of heat on this. Homicide wants to take five names off the board by charging Falcone. The brass is satisfied this is a closed loop."

The room was one of many used for interviews on her wing of the Bureau's office suites. Marsha had turned the chairs around the roundtable to be facing one another across the small round Formica table so that they had equal access to the door. It was kept entirely devoid of artwork, posters or knickknacks. Beige walls and thin dark-brown coffee-stained carpets completed the ambiance of a government's typical interview room. Most "guests" would rather be outside of the door that did have a glass panel running length-wise.

"And what do you think, Mike?"

"Oh no, I defer to your deductive reasoning powers. Your brother said you were real police."

"Thanks, Mike, and the same goes for you. Nicky says you're real police too." Pedigree asked and answered, she accepted the invitation to show her card first. "I wonder how a brand new luxury car's brake lights aren't working at the same time that all the evidence to send him away for life is sitting in the trunk."

Mike nodded his head. "Yeah, we agree on that point, but here's one more. Vice got a tip he was hot, and the uniforms waited until he was a couple blocks away from his house before making the minor equipment violation car stop."

New info. Marsha nodded. "Whoever put the goodies in the trunk disabled the brake lights and tipped you off."

"Yeah, but nobody wants to hear that Giggy is an innocent man."

The unmistakable hum of office life carried through the open door. Phones rang, workers walked by with binders or staring down earnestly at cell phones. No one was paying attention to their conversation. It was just another day of business for the FBI.

"Well, he's only innocent of this," Marsha agreed with the unspoken quandary that you sometimes take down a bad guy when you get the chance, while the real doer is still out free and clear to commit more violence.

Mike shifted uncomfortably on his plastic chair. A big guy, but his suit was cut to hide it well, Marsha observed.

"I guess that is why I'm here. My people want this to go away, but I can't help but think that was just the opening salvo in a war that has exploded."

"Talking about explosions, ATF's bomb people say that the detonating devices and explosives from all three bombs were identical, with two of the payloads being white phosphorus and the other anti-personnel." Marsha flipped her card over.

"So in round two, we see another guy getting pinned for the bombings," Mike said.

"What do you see as the connection?" As soon as she said it, she reached over to the report on the car that was bombed in South Philly. Once she acquired its photo and reg plate, she went sifting through the raw images taken by the newbie at the wake.

Mike drank from the styrofoam cup of still hot and acidic all-day cop coffee.

She laid the photos she found down side by side to the pictures of the bombed-out car.

"This car was sitting in the parking lot at Renko's Funeral Home." She didn't feel the need to say anything about the apparent match.

As Mike leaned in to look at the photos, Marsha leaned back and drank from her cup.

"Military precision. This isn't homegrown talent. Some group is either paying for an out of town hitter, or we have a really bad actor walking around in plain sight," he said.

"Fuckin' ay."

"Yo, fuckin' ay is right," Mike acknowledged.

They sat with this hypothesis for a while, churning the combinations and permutations through their own minds. This is what real police do; didn't matter that he is a cop and I work for the FBI, Marsha thought.

She shuffled her photographs in a large circle on the table. "Let me kill a Russian, a collateral, three Jamaicans, two South Philly made men, the local leadership of the Dominicans and a Columbian soldier in eight days after the Old Man croaks." Marsha was first. She took an index card and wrote OLD MAN on it and placed it to the outside of the circle, next to Yury Yukolov.

"I want to start a war where I get everybody fighting each other," Mike added. He filled out the circle with photos that came out of his tabbed accordion folder.

"Let's not forget the gangbangers mimicking the action," Marsha added. She placed their photos in a larger ring around the first group.

"Yeah, it started with the Old Man, then all hell broke loose," Mike concluded.

"One second, Mike." Marsha reached for her cell phone. "Hey, Ramit can you….. Yes, I am fine Ramit, how are you?" Marsha rolled her eyes and shook her head. "That's nice. Can you print off 5x8s of the Russians that went to the Old Man's wake with a little something about them on a separate sheet?"

Then to Mike, she said, "I thought we might as well look at the living Russians to see if anything clicks."

Marsha liked that she and Mike kept batting ideas around; some were wild-ass guesses while others had merit. They didn't have to be on the same page, but at least they were reading from the same book.

Ramit arrived quickly, pushing a large cork board/whiteboard on wheels. "Um Agent, uh Marsha, here are the photos of the all the Russians that went into the wake. I borrowed the situation board if you needed it."

Marsha didn't want to consider the situation board right now and especially in front of an outsider.

"Ramit Ravikant, allow me to introduce you to Philly Homicide Detective Sgt. Michael Hollins."

Both men nodded to each other.

Ramit gave a short synopsis for each man that came in to pay his respects as he laid down the man's photo.

"I recognize this guy. God, it had to be ten years ago. He beat a rap for moving hot cars out in shipping containers. I busted him when I worked the Joint Auto Theft Task Force. What the hell was his name?"

Ramit connected the photo to his list and said," Arkady Valnikov, AV Exporting." He rattled off a Delaware Avenue address in Bridesburg.

"Yeah, that's right. I remember now. How can you ever forget the ones that get away?" Mike said.

They all stared at the picture for a minute then Ramit continued to lay down the rest of the photos.

Mike said, "For a nobody, the Old Man had a ton of friends."

Marsha watched and listened. After all the photos were set out. She stared at them and asked Ramit, "What about the Vlad character?"

Ramit was puzzled.

Marsha pulled up the photo of Vladislav Balderis.

"Why isn't he on the table?" she asked.

"You asked me to retrieve the photos of the Russians that went into the wake. He stayed outside with all the drivers and bodyguards."

Mike flipped the phone around to see the photo. "That's a serious looking dude." Then the picture timed out, and they went back to the photos on the conference table.

Marsha arranged the Russians in a circle around the Old Man. Leave it on the table, and this exercise was just that, an exercise. Looking at a large empty situation board, she knew in her gut that she had to put them up there, but with that move, her intelligence would become actionable, and that meant work, lots of work.

Mike and Ramit watched silently as Marsha looked back and forth from the table to the empty cork board. She got up and said. "Give me a hand and let's put these up on the board."

When they were done, they stood back and stared at it. Mike was the first to speak, "Let's pay my old pal a visit. I am sure he will be happy to see me again." He walked up to the board and pulled Arkady's photo from the group.

Marsha said, "Mike and Marsha's Excellent Adventure." Realizing that Ramit felt left out, she said, "Don't worry, Ramit. We will need you too."

Several miles north on Sixth Street and a few blocks over, Vlad and the accountant finished their day of collections and bribes. Vlad parked next to the Old Man's rowhouse and let the accountant out. Their conversations were no more and no less than usual. The accountant made his way up the stairs and placed his key in the door. His was the only other key besides the Old Man's. He took the money and ledger book to the floor safe hidden in the basement. This safe was more expensive than most of the houses on the block. He turned to find Vlad standing there.

Vlad grabbed the accountant by his raincoat lapel and hissed at him, "Where's the video?"

CHAPTER TEN

B*e Careful What You Ask For*
By Stew Menke

Car bombs, two taps to the head, drug money rip-offs. Seems just like when things were getting boring on the crime beat, the underworld surfaces with a hit parade that this city hasn't seen since Dick Clark's American Bandstand.

The headlines blare: "Killer's Gun Is Tied To 5 Executions." "Home-made Bombs Go Off In Three Different Parts Of The City Within Hours, Terrorism Ruled Out." Who is responsible? What started the mayhem? I know my articles have done an excellent job on the bottom of your birdcages for years and for keeping your hoagie from dripping all over your lap while you sit in traffic, but I never thought my columns would wake a sleeping bear.

Philadelphia's finest and the good folks at the FBI are mum on the subject. "Under investigation," my tight-lipped sources tell me. It's easier to steal gold from Fort Knox than get a decent quote on this.

Your favorite writer is at a loss to explain why so many tribes are on the warpath. So I will trudge to the press conferences and listen to the assurances that the general public is not the target; that the recipients of these surgical strikes were decided in advance and were taken out with prejudice.

Giovanni "Giggy" Falcone is screaming that he was set up in the alleged murders of a strip club manager and dancer along with three reputed members of a Jamaican street gang. No bond was set, and he remains sequestered for his own protection.

The bombings, I'm told, all bear the signature of the same maker believed to be a Columbian national, Edgar Cabrera, who died when his last bomb turned his own car into a crematory. And it looks like things are heating up elsewhere. Street level shootings are now erupting in turf wars. Nobody was prepared for this increase in organized crime and gang warfare. It doesn't appear that any neighborhood is immune from this rampage.

Just last night, a fast and furious chase down Kelly Drive ended up with one car crashing into Boat House Row and the other taking a chilly dip in the Schuylkill.

Why here, why now, and more importantly, when does it end?

Stew sent the column off to his editor minutes before the deadline, but four hours after the lottery numbers were announced. It was the second day in a row of not seeing the numbers from Sparrow in the blog comments of the website that was bookmarked on the Chromebook. The column was more of an attempt to let this Vlad character think that he was clueless. He wanted more time to decide how to break the story with this video that he watched every day since the accountant brought it to him. Hell, he didn't even know Sparrow's name. He didn't like having the damn thing in his apartment, and he wanted to be rid of it. He yanked out the thumb drive and hid it where nobody would find it. Convinced he waited too long, Stew did the next best thing. He dialed a number he had on his Rolodex of stapled business cards.

"Hello, Special Agent O'Shea, this is Stew Menke from *The Daily Sun*. I would really appreciate it if you gave me a call back when you get this at 215-555-3456." He paused and added, "I have urgent business to discuss with you."It would be another long night of chain-smoking and staring out the window of his third-floor apartment halfway between the college he graduated from and the shrine of his childhood, Connie Mack Stadium, long since torn down.

CHAPTER ELEVEN

S tew was uncharacteristically quiet on the ride back to his apartment, Sully thought.

"What up Stew? You hardly said anything while we served and afterward. Trying to figure out who the Eagles are gonna draft?"

"No, Sully, thinking of all these mob hits." The sports talk guys and listeners were grinding away on who the Eagles needed in the upcoming college draft. He leaned over and turned down the volume.

"Yeah, another shooting last night," Sully said referring to the Columbian social club where two masked guys wearing bullet-proof vests and toting machine guns riddled the entrance killing three and wounding eight. It was all caught on tape and was continuously repeated on the news cycle all day. As Sully walked by the banks and convenience stores, he could see the story being played out over and over again.

"No doubt retaliation for the bombing at the Dominican's dance club the other night," Stew replied.

They made their way up the stairs to Stew's apartment. "Let me put some coffee on, while I check the scores." Stew disappeared into his stand-up kitchen. Sully never tired at discovering new delights from Stew's collection of signed photographs.

"Where was that taken?" said Sully gazing at a picture of Stew with Willie Mays both in tux and bow ties.

"New York Sports Writers Banquet," came the terse reply from the kitchen, where Stew was lingering over a Chromebook. Sully could see Stew shaking his head.

"New computer, Stew?"

"No money for raises, but sometimes working for a major Metro paper does have its perks. They want us to be more efficient." Stew grabbed a canvas bag and placed the charger and laptop in it. "How about I make it a birthday present for you?"

"How'd you know it was my birthday?"

"You told me a long time ago?"

It was just another thing that Sully didn't remember saying. "Gee, thanks, I won't keep it where I sleep. Things have a way of walking, even though it's pretty safe there.

Sully and Stew had been there once when Stew insisted on dropping him off. Western Terminal was in the forgotten part of Philly's waterfront and served as an encampment for the homeless vets.

Access was limited by two checkpoints at either end of the trucking terminal and abandoned warehouse. A collection of old RVs, box trucks, and mini-vans served the more squared away vets, or the "working poor" as people liked to call them. F Troop was a more colorful name that got picked up by the press for the gathering. Sully had a surplus tent under the loading dock that was dry and shielded from the wind blowing off the Delaware in sight of the Tacony Palmyra bridge.

Stew walked back into the kitchen and brought out two steaming 1980 Phillies World Series mugs, creamers and sugar packets. Sully dumped enough cream and sugar into his cup to turn the coffee tan.

Sully spotted a baseball bat by the door, put down his mug and picked it the bat. "Spring training?"

"No, just a little spooked about this mob stuff since I started writing about it."

Sully picked it up and ran his hand over the barrel.

"It's signed by Joe DiNatale," Stew said, "Yeah, he gave it to me when I quit being a beat writer for the Phillies. We stay in touch."

Sully took a couple of natural swings, remembering what it was like to play baseball growing up and wanting to be a big leaguer. He put it back by the door and turned around to see Stew handing him another present. This one was wrapped. "Promise me you won't open it until your birthday."

"Sure, Stew." It had been a few years since anybody gave him a present of any sort.

They sat in comfortable silence, but Sully saw that Stew was elsewhere.

Stew surprised him when he said, "Coming back from war is hard and harder on some than most. It's not easy to admit that as much as you want to leave the war behind, it doesn't let you forget. It keeps turning your world into crap. You cannot put your finger on why something is wrong with you, because you don't know what it is. Then your luck goes from bad to worse. Before you know it, you're over your head."

Here comes the lecture, Sully thought. But instead, Stew said, "I have faith in you, and I know you can do it."

Sully couldn't remember the last time that somebody said he could do something right, and more importantly, that somebody believed in him. His family had given up on him. His wife told him to get out, and he hadn't seen his daughter in over two years. Stew was his only friend and here was Stew saying that he could do it.

At first, the words came out tentatively, but then came out in a flood, "You're right, Stew. I have to figure this out for myself. You know, I think I can go back to my tent tonight and tomorrow talk to some of the other guys about how they got started." With that, the two men got up and shook hands.

It was awkward. Stew was first to speak. "Semper Fi, soldier."

"Semper Fi, Stew." Sully took his present and the bag and headed to the door. He got to the entrance vestibule and reached for the door as a large student wearing a Temple sweatsuit opened the door, and Sully bumped into him. "Sorry, kid," Sully said. The student had his hoodie up and probably was wearing headphones and didn't hear him, Sully thought.

When he hit the street, Sully pulled his coat lapels up and his Flyers knit hat down and started his trek back to Western Terminal. It was cold, but the coffee had warmed him up. A few minutes later, he felt the pull to go into the pharmacy and stood there as the automatic door opened and closed. Then he felt the urge and loitered by the liquor store for the college kids, then he walked past it. Semper Fi, Stew.

CHAPTER TWELVE

W as that bum ever going to leave? Vlad thought as he walked up the stairs. The retaliation killings were starting as he hoped, but he needed to keep adding fuel to the fire. This change in plans was not anticipated. At the second-floor landing, he listened for the sounds of other occupants. The first floor was quiet, and from the mailboxes, it confirmed that the second floor was vacant. From his surveillance positions across the street, he had observed no movement. No lights had come on or gone off on that floor.

He had improvised on many special operations when the intel was wrong, or things didn't work out as planned. There was more risk here than he liked, but what choice did he have? Finding out about the hidden video feed from the club had reminded him that even the best plans have flaws. His source told him that a rookie crime scene tech had spotted the pinhole camera and microphone. Using the same kind of equipment that he possessed, they were able to find the transmitter, power it up and tell to what IP address it was sending the signal. When they executed the warrant on the Old Man's row house, they found the laptop in his bedroom.

Fortunately, the day of his visit to the club had been erased.

He chided himself for not taking better precautions. Unfortunately, the forensic examination showed that an external drive received the missing video before it was deleted from the hard drive. He should have known that the VIP room was a virtual voyeur's paradise.

In his arrogance, he wanted Yury to see the face of "Bad Vlad" before killing him; however, this country still had the death penalty for organized crime killings on the federal level.

Here he stood at the last place where he knew that video was located. He had to find out if he could retrieve it or if he had to start running immediately. He had his getaway kit and a list of countries that do not have extradition treaties with America. Killing mobsters with international connections gave him more concern. He might have to disappear so that no one could find him. There was a hunting camp deep in the Urals. Extradition would be favorable.

He lightly knocked on the apartment door. The apartment door had no peephole. He didn't want to force the door and make it look like a home invasion unless he had to. He had a serviceable pre-text as a student wishing to rent the vacant second-floor apartment.

"What's the matter, Sully, you forget something?" Menke asked as he opened the door.

Vlad pushed his way in. He saw the look of recognition on the man's face. He saw him glance at the baseball bat. He picked it up in his gloved hand by the barrel and began poking the handle into the frail man's chest backing him up till he stumbled onto the ratty couch. Vlad lifted his hoodie and baseball cap from over his eyes and glared down at Menke on the sofa.

"Semper Fi," Menke said.

"What does that mean?" Vlad moved in closer.

"It means fuck you asshole." Menke spit out.

Vlad tapped Menke a few times on the cheek with the bat handle. "I have broken stronger men than you, old man."

"I know your name, Vlad. I've been dealing with bullies all my life. I never backed down before, and I am not backing down now."

Vlad thrust the bat handle into Menke's solar plexus knocking the wind out of him. Menke bent forward and Vlad grabbed a handful of his sweater and slammed him into the coffee table scattering books and a butt-filled glass ashtray. He now straddled Menke as he lay face down on the cheap carpet. He knelt down with his left knee digging into the middle of the short and thin man's back.

He waited until Menke regained his breath. "Where is it?"

"Semper Fi."

Vlad pinned Stew's right hand to the floor and separated Stew's fingers with his own knuckles till the little finger was painfully splayed out. "Last chance."

"Semper Fi," came the reply.

Vlad flipped the bat around and mashed the top of the barrel down on the finger, breaking it. Menke's scream was extinguished when Vlad's knee compressed the reporter's rib cage.

Vlad repeated the mashing with each finger. Menke passed out when Vlad broke his thumb.

Vlad lifted the quivering body to a kitchen chair like a rag doll and secured the now-limp elderly man to the chair with zip ties he had kept in his sweater pouch.

He started tossing the living room, walking around the limp rag-doll figure, until he saw Menke coming to. Vlad sat on a turned around chair facing Menke. "You decide how you will die. Just tell me where it is, and it will be painless, or we can keep doing this. I have all night, and you are not going anywhere."

Stew gagged and lowered his head, mumbling.

"What?"

Stew mumbled again.

Vlad leaned in, "Tell me."

Stew lifted his head and spit blood and phlegm from internal injuries directly into Vlad's face. "Semper. Fi."

Vlad exploded in rage. He swung the bat into Menke's head with such force that the impact sounded like the time he and his friends destroyed a farmer's melon patch with uprooted fence posts. Over and over again, Vlad swung downwards, sideways left to right and then back. Menke's face became a purplish mash of blood, bone and loose skin. Death came slowly and mercilessly.

He didn't stop beating the battered body with the baseball bat until his hands ached. Blood spattered all over his tracksuit and gloves touched off memories from when he chased resistance fighters in Georgia. His seething rage continued as he spiraled back in his mind to that early fall day with his team.

A welding shop owner pled with Vlad. He adamantly denied that he had any involvement with the rebels outfitting their open-bed trucks with mounted machine guns. Vlad was convinced that the man allowed them to use his equipment. Vlad was using tin snips to remove the man's fingers of his right hand at the middle knuckles, but the torture was not getting the desired results.

As Vlad was about to lope off the man's right thumb, the man yelled, "Fuck your mother!" in his own dialect, then he spit in Vlad's face. Vlad saw red and began slashing the man with twin blades of the snips. His team had to pull him away from the shop owner whose throat was slashed to bloody ribbons.

Vlad's blood pounding in his temples subsided, and he saw that he was not in the back room of a welding shop, but in a threadbare apartment in North Philadelphia.

He gathered his breath slowly and cursed the body sagging against the restraints. His anger finally dissipated. He nudged

Menke's head up with the end of the bat and watched it drop down like a rag doll.

Vlad was left with the realization that once again, he let a nobody push his buttons. He cut the bloody zip ties with his knife and collected them. As he regained his composure, he systematically finished tossing the apartment.

The adrenaline surge was draining off, and he was feeling the effects of his exertion. He was looking for a needle in the haystack. Cereal boxes were spilled into the sink. Frozen packages were ripped open and any loose floorboard was pried up. Vlad became more frustrated at his failure to find what he came for. Neither the Chromebook, nor the thumb drive was present.

He was sure the accountant had not lied to him. Vlad listened for noises in the hallway. Students could still be lingering there after a night of partying. He returned his cap and hoodie to cover his scowling frustration as he closed the door behind him. As he descended the stairs, the adrenaline released from his system. He was left with a calm, clear voice that cried out to him what he had to do next.

He recalled the bum Sully. What was he carrying when he left? The cops or the newspapers do not have the tape yet. I have to find it before they get it.

CHAPTER THIRTEEN

The heavy equipment and delivery trucks backing up at nearby industrial sites were his alarm clock. It was still, and the sunlight streamed into the seams of his tent. The Polar XZ sleeping bag did its job, and he was still dry. It's amazing how nice waking up can be without wondering if you shit or pissed yourself. No blinding headache either. He could get used to this.

He nodded to Checkpoint Charlie. Charlie nodded back. "Morning, Sully."

A quick hot shower and a clean change of clothes were a good start. If he could make it in time for the lunch serving at All Saints, he could down some grease to slow down the shakes. A sober reminder that he was a stone-cold alcoholic. Maybe he'd stay for the AA big book meeting and try to connect with a sponsor. As he walked the mile or so of Delaware Avenue towards the church, he replayed his conversation with Stew in his mind. I'm gonna do it this time, Stew. Semper Fi.

The school next to the church had been closed for years due to declining inner-city enrollments and found new life as both a senior and child daycare center. At one time, this was the gymnasium for the grade school. He spotted some of the regulars and sat quietly with the group that would lead the meeting afterward. They would get the room ready for the change-over, and soon enough, he volunteered to help. Opening a locked cabinet where the coffee urns and cookies were kept, the meeting leader stared at the empty cupboard after pulling down the urns.

"Oh shit, there will be a riot if we don't have any cookies." Strong coffee and sugary cookies were meeting room staples.

"I'll go," Sully said. The leader reached into his pocket, and Sully shook his head and patted his own pocket.

Sully double-timed it to the nearest quick-mart and was loaded down with the cheapest and largest bags of sugar cookies. He waited for the clerk to punch in every conceivable lottery ticket game for the senior citizen trying to create his retirement fund from the scratch-offs. Sully glanced up at the TV monitor above and to the right of the counter and then screamed at the clerk, "Turn that up!"

"I can't. The boss said no sound on in store."

The close-captioning was slowly catching up with the video. Sully had to wait for the newscaster to finish talking about what happened to discover the horrible truth about the grisly findings in North Philadelphia. The graphic now was of an aerial map of the location of a three-story row house apartment building halfway between Temple University and where the Church campus that occupied the former lot of Connie Mack Stadium stood. The newscaster went on to describe the man found dead there of an apparent robbery. Stew's iconic photographs of locker room interviews with ballplayers flashed across the screen. While the close-captioning continued, the one picture that remained on the screen was of Stew wearing his signature Frank Sinatra 50's era hat with a cigarette dangling from his lips pecking away at a typewriter in the press box of Veteran's Stadium.

"Sir, you're holding up the line," the clerk demanded. Sully looked at him and looked back at the screen. He dumped the cookies on the counter and peeled off a twenty from his inside his thin roll of cash and dropped it on the counter. He backed off from the counter mesmerized by the last of the report. The clerk handed him the bags and his change. He mechanically stuffed the money back in his coat. Walking back to the meeting was dizzying. Sully had to stop twice to get his bearings. The images of the apartment location and Stew's photos began to blur. He was not walking fast but had to stop to catch his breath. He stumbled into the meeting with the graceful gait of a zombie. He handed the bag to the leader who gave him a puzzled look.

Sully said, "You know the old guy I help out at the soup kitchen?" The leader nodded. Others formed a line by the coffee urn that was percolating nicely and were waiting expectantly for the cookies to be put out. They looked at Sully.

"I was with him last night. I was probably the last person to see him alive." For a brief second, Sully flashed to the college kid that looked and walked like a linebacker.

In most groups that formed for myriad reasons, this revelation would come as shock, but for those gathering for this meeting, sudden and violent death was sadly a regular topic of discussion.

Sully retreated from the converted gym; the anxiety and claustrophobia strangling him. He felt as though the cold winter sun was blinding him. He turned away. The sunspots were widening. He pulled at his parka zipper and the cold air rushed onto his heaving chest. He couldn't catch his breath. He staggered to a stop on a street he didn't recognize. The all too familiar darkness started closing in. Here we go again. The roar in his ears quickly overtook his mind and then his body. Everything went black.

CHAPTER FOURTEEN

Jospeh Sullivan woke up in a hospital bed. The intravenous drip attached to his arm was the first thing he noticed. Then he looked over to the other side of the bed to see two well-dressed men and an equally well-dressed woman standing over him. He tried sitting up, but the rush to his head almost caused him to pass out. That is when a blinding headache caused his eyes to tear, and he was close to vomiting. He gagged once and realized that his diaphragm was sore from the same reflexive actions. He must have thrown up a lot from the last thing he remembered until now. He passed out again.

He regained consciousness to the blinding light in one eye. It was removed, and he then saw a doctor at the other end of the penlight.

"You are one lucky hombre, Mr. Sullivan. If a dog didn't break off his leash and stay with you until its owner found you behind a skating rink, you would have frozen to death."

"What? Where?" is all Sully could manage through his parched and cracking lips.

"Two days ago."

"What day is it?"

"Why it is actually your birthday, Mr. Sullivan. Happy birthday. You almost didn't get to celebrate it."

Sully sunk back into the hospital bed. Six days ago, he had been handed his birthday presents by Stew. Stew was killed that night. Two days in the hospital meant three to four days in a blackout. That's about par for the course. *Fuckin' asshole.*

"Some police detectives want to talk to you. They came by yesterday for a while, but you weren't ready to talk to anybody."

"What about?"

"You'll have to ask them. Before, I let them back in here, I should mention that it was a good thing that you almost froze to death."

Sully looked at him, waiting for the other shoe to drop.

"Because the low temperatures slowed down your heart rate, respiration and metabolism. No frostbite either. We were able to detox you from alcohol poisoning. Your blood alcohol was off the chart. If it were July and not January, the dog would have found your corpse. I'll come back and check on you after they leave."

The cops came back into the room. Sully's relationships with police had soured in the last couple of years. The police had given him his nickname, "Listerine Man." He could remember getting poked in the ribs one too many times as a wakeup when he had passed out on the streets or on a park bench.

"How are you feeling, Mr. Sullivan?" the woman asked.

"Never been better. How about you?"

"You had quite a scare there," she said without missing a beat.

"So I've been told. What brings you here? I am sure it is not to discuss my general health. Do you mind me asking for some ID? Most times it's guys in uniforms that get up in my face."

"Marsha O'Shea, FBI." She flashed her credentials.

"Detective Sgt. Michael Hollins," he said, as he slid his business cards across the small credenza holding Sully's sipper bottle.

Sully grabbed it and stared at his. "Organized Crime Unit."

"Detective Wes Thompson. Homicide." Thompson was not smiling and sat with his hands folded across his stomach, making no move to otherwise identify himself.

Sully closed his eyes and tried to process this information. He didn't know what meds they had pumped into his system, but just as his anxiety started to rise, he felt a warmth flood his body emanating out from his chest to his extremities. Suddenly, he felt exhausted. He wanted to open his eyes and look at them to say something, but he was overwhelmed with sleepiness.

"Mr. Sullivan?" Marsha asked.

"Mr. Sullivan?" Mike Hollins asked.

"Shit. Not again." Thompson complained.

The doctor was in the room in less than 30 seconds. "All right everybody, my patient won't be answering any questions for a while. If you want to return to the waiting room, I'll have someone come and fetch you when he's awake."

Marsha slipped her card into Sully's hospital gown pocket.

CHAPTER FIFTEEN

"Sounds to me like a straight up robbery that went bad," Drummond Sr. added.

"No forced entry," Marsha replied.

"Not the first time that a vic invited the killer in. Maybe somebody he knew," Marsha's father replied from the head of the dining room table in the Drummond family home.

"No other motive," Nick chimed in.

"No defensive wounds," Marsha countered and anted. "Medical examiner says he was tortured."

"The do-er wanted to know where he kept his stash of cash. That's all. Sounds like a druggie to me, honey," Dad countered.

"Yeah, Sis, you can't look at that neighborhood and ignore the percentages," Nick added.

Marsha looked at the two men in her life. Both had way more experience investigating street violence then she did at the Bureau, but she knew the death they were discussing was not yet another North Philly senseless murder, where bodies dropped on a regular basis for even less cause. Covet a man's woman, you get shot. Steal a teen's bicycle, you get stabbed to death. Drug rip-off retaliations were common. Life there seemed cheapened by the senseless brutality.

"No, this was a crime beat reporter who just happened to be investigating organized crime before a shooting war started and was killed because he knew something. Didn't matter if it was the ghetto or Society Hill. Stew Menke got offed because the killer wanted him silenced," Marsha said.

Nick was first to respond. "Does the FBI want to Bigfoot this case or is it something personal, Agent O'Shea?"

Marsha bristled at the thought that she was stepping all over the locals on this case. "Actually, Captain Drummond, my employer would rather see me gathering intelligence on all the mob-related killings and take a back seat to your Homicide unit on this one. My squad went from sleep-walking through a nice pre-retirement gig to have to do real police work. Nobody here is happy with my harping on this. Oh, Homicide Detective Thompson wants me to, and I quote, 'stop shitting in his sandbox.'"

"So, Marsha, why are you tilting at windmills?" her dad asked.

"Because everything that I've ever been taught tells me that Stew Menke's death is the key."

"You need to back off and let the murder police do their thing," Nick said.

"Yeah, Marsha, it won't be long before they ID the perp, you'll see."

And on cue, Marsha's mother delivered the Sunday roast to the table. "Who is going to say grace?" she said, effectively ending the cop talk.

Marsha brooded over her disagreement with her father and brother but engaged in the conversation with her family. No husband, no kids, no nieces or nephews, no boyfriend to speak of —this was her center. Where would she be without them? After her divorce and being alone in Miami, she steeped too much in loneliness. Her bed saw too many one-nighters.

She helped her mom clear the dinner plates and put candles on her dad's birthday cake. They walked out the kitchen singing "Happy Birthday," and Nick joined in. The cake was placed in front of her father, and he blew out the candles. Soon her mom was cutting portions that were bigger than any person should eat, while Marsha scooped vanilla ice cream. Soon the sugar soothed away all the troubles, and for the rest of the meal, Marsha was able to just be a daughter and sister.

Nick's birthday card was a hit. Her mom's gift of socks was warmly received. Marsha reached down into the large rectangular shopping bag with string-wrapped handles and said, "Close your eyes, Pop."

"C'mon, Marsha, I don't like surprises," he said.

She kept her hand in the bag and said, "I know dad, close your eyes."

"All right, dear."

She surprised her dad with gifts for as long as she could remember. She was happy that most of the surprises she gave her father were pleasant. She pulled the framed front page of the now defunct *Philadelphia Bulletin* displaying a photo of a lean, tall, and good-looking patrolman leading two disheveled handcuffed thugs from a Girard Bank. The two-inch headline read. "POLICE FOIL BANK ROBBERY, NO ONE HURT"

She showed it to her brother and mother before telling him, "Okay, open your eyes."

As he opened his eyes, he took in the memory. He immediately began to tear up. "Oh, Marsha, you shouldn't have."

Nicholas Drummond Sr. pushed his chair back from the table and tilted the frame so that the glass gave no glare and slowly whistled to himself. "My proudest moment." He gave a glance to Nick and looked down and away from the women, before breathing deeply. "Of course, I had just met your mother and hadn't asked her to marry me yet."

"Oh, honey." Marsha's mother gave her husband's shoulders a hug from behind as she too admired the man in the photo.

Marsha could see the look in their eyes and tried to imagine them as young romancers.

Nick broke the quiet, tender moment first and said, "Way to hit it out of the park, Sis."

Differences and disappointments were forgotten or at least suspended for those few glorious minutes in the Drummond household. Things returned to normal soon enough, lest anybody stay too sentimental too long. In short order, Marsha was kissing and hugging her parents on her way out the door.

Three hours later, the barkeeper at Delahanty's came back to the table by the unused shuffleboard and began collecting the empty shot glasses and pitcher in front of her. "The cab's outside waiting for you, Marsha," he said with a soft but firm County Cork brogue.

At first, she got angry. She tried to stand up and fell back into the chair. She waited for the room to stop spinning. When it did, she opened her eyes. He was nodding to her with the realization that he made the right call. She took his hand in resignation, and he helped her to her feet.

On the cab ride home, the telephone message that she was listening to again and again hadn't changed at all after Ramit had undeleted it from the system a few days earlier. Oh, how she wished it was different. That message and the alcohol fueled her self-loathing even more. Her friends Jimmy Beam and Bud Weiser had been there to keep her company, and now in her stupor, two things remained crystal clear: First, all I had to do was listen to the whole fucking message, and that reporter would still be alive. The second was, I'll never tell my family that I screwed up, ever.

She tipped the cabbie at her Fairmount section townhouse. She trudged to the bedroom shedding clothes as she stumbled down the hall to her bathroom. As she knelt before the commode waiting for the inevitable climax to her stupidity, she flashed back to the young cop in the photograph. He had no radio, no backup, and no bulletproof vest. Carrying only a standard issue four-inch .38 cal Smith and Wesson revolver and outgunned, he convinced two desperados to drop their weapons and surrender. He didn't walk away from his duty and neither will I. I will find Menke's killer.

CHAPTER SIXTEEN

"You have to wait until he's released."

"I pay you for better answers than that," Vlad said.

The source folded his arms and shook his head. "What? You expect some *Mission Impossible* shit? Sneak into the hospital and while no one is watching, administer the truth serum and have him tell us where he hid the video?"

"His tent is clean?" Vlad asked.

"He kept nothing there except his clothes and his sleeping bag. We tossed it."

Word came back from the Twenty-sixth police district that Sullivan lived with other homeless veterans along the Delaware in an encampment where they pretty much policed themselves. The collection of rusted out RVs, tents, and lean-tos on an abandoned factory's loading dock had earned the nickname "F Troop."

"So where does he stash his valuables?" Vlad persisted.

"We are asking that same question. We all want something to tie Sullivan to the murder. My higher-ups want Sullivan for it too. They don't want to open up Pandora's Box and say that a crime reporter was killed for reporting on organized crime. That is bad Ju-Ju. There are still crusading investigative journalists with blog followings who will swarm on this town like locusts. They will be followed by the cable news idiots and tabloids; that is if it's a slow week in celebrity break-ups. The fourth estate has to act like they can't allow one of their own to be killed for doing real journalism."

"What about the FBI?"

"What about them? They are too busy chasing down every terrorist lead. Something about not wanting to have another 9-11 on their watch."

It was payday for this source, and Vlad was making him jump through hoops like a circus lion. "Every day I wake up wondering if today is the day that the video surfaces," Vlad said.

The two stood in silence watching the barges being pushed up and down the river. The battleship USS *New Jersey* was moored on the Camden side. They had bought their tickets for the tour of the USS *Olympia*, a Spanish-American era battleship permanently docked on the Philly side. They veered off from the cub scout packs and leaned over the railings next to the gun turrets. No cameras, no recording devices on this turn of the previous century vessel allowed them the privacy for a rare face-to-face.

The source said, "I can buy you three or four hours of running time. From now on, you should use a hotel, just in case."

Vlad said, "The accountant told me what he did with it. The reporter did not use it and died a horrible death rather than tell me who had it, knowing what fate awaited them. This bum was so out of it, he probably doesn't even know that he has it. Kill him, and it stops there."

"The hospital is too risky. Cameras, police going in an out all the time, and his connection to the reporter are too many vari-ables. You can't control any part of the scene or the timing. If we arrest him for the murder, he gets a lawyer who works his defense that the victim was tortured because he was promising a Mob expose. You might get a private eye snooping around and gets lucky stumbling across the video. No, he has to be released from the hospital, and he has to disappear. We get to clear the case without an arrest. My bosses can go back to worrying about the next catastrophe, and the hordes of journalists will never materialize."

"How do you suggest we make that happen?" Vlad asked.

"What do you mean 'we?'"

"The good news is that you are getting a raise." Vlad slid the thicker than normal envelope into the pocket of the source's knee-length black leather coat. "The bad news is the accountant told me that he copied the pay-off list into a spreadsheet and added it to thumb-drive."

"How much?"

"From the beginning."

CHAPTER SEVENTEEN

So much had changed since their last monthly meeting. Arkady Valnikov looked around the table. In the cramped dining room of the Old Man's row house, the group was much larger but felt so much smaller without the accountant, Yury, and the Old Man. Worse, he didn't like what he was seeing and hearing. Each of the six remaining lieutenants had been assigned Vlad's old Special Forces buddies as bodyguards.

How dare that punk sit at the table, the balls he has to sit in the Old Man's spot. "You were with the accountant on the last collection day, where is he? Why haven't we heard from him? What happened to him, Vlad?" Arkady shot the questions like arrows.

"Belize." Vlad replied.

How dare he smugly grunt at us with a two-syllable answer? They sat in silence until Leonid caved in.

"How do we know that the pay-offs are being made with our money?"

"As I told you before, the rules have changed. I rode with him on all his stops, and he gave me the ledger book and combination to the safe before I dropped him off at his apartment. I will see that your businesses and your personal protection are taken care of. I will take over the accountant's duties. From now on, your fees for my services will go to these accounts. I have contracted with an off-shore accountant to monitor our arrangements."

Simultaneously, their smartphones pinged with an inbound message. They all stared at instructions for the crypto-currency payments.

Vlad added, "Before you begin whining and complaining about the increase, each of you will share with me in Yury's take from the gentlemen clubs and sports bars. Your additional costs for protection are more than covered by your split of Yury's net."

Arkady was not convinced that Vlad would step up and take over at the clubs. "Who is going to assume Yury's day-to-day operations?" It now was clear to Arkady that the others would not challenge Bad Vlad. The vision of the closed casket and knowing that Yury was shot in his penis before his face was destroyed was a clear message to them all.

"Boris from Atlantic City will take over for half of my take, and he is happy for it. In return, he will pass on video to me of anybody from our town that gets naughty in his VIP rooms. You see, Arkady, I am growing our wealth and capital."

Arkady snorted. "Don't tell me it's raining when you are pissing on my leg, Vlad. Belize, really? I think you dropped the accountant at Departures to the Netherworld. We didn't decide how to deal with Yury's businesses. You made the decision on your own, without consulting us. What makes y——."

"Unless you haven't noticed, Arkady, we are in a war to protect what is ours. Not one of you have talked to me about retribution for Yury's murder. His family had to have a closed casket. What about that? Tell me what you plan to make the Sicilians pay for this?"

The two men were locked in a stare down. Vlad slowly rose to his feet from the table where he had invited himself to sit.

"The killing has to stop, not escalate Vlad. The Old Man taught us how to stand down when our emotions ran hot. No one has talked to any of the groups involved in all the killings. In times of war, diplomacy is even more important. It's getting worse and not better."

"Diplomacy is just another word for appeasement. You six are not willing to fight for what the Old Man worked hard to take. He made you all rich beyond imagination. That is why, in my respect for the Old Man and what he would have wished for, you will be protected by me, but you will not stand in my way as I take care of Yury's killers and take what we want from the others."

"The reporter, Vlad, I want to know who killed him." Arkady shifted to his real reason for making Vlad angry.

Vlad reeled from the question. "What do you mean?"

"What do our sources tell us why the reporter was killed?" Arkady insisted.

"It was some street bum that worked with him at a soup kitchen down on your Waterfront, Arkady. He was looking for cash, I am told."

"Then why was I questioned by the police department and the FBI yesterday?"

Vlad slammed the plaster wall just missing the Byzantine painting of the Holy Mother and Infant, causing Leonid to duck. "Why didn't you report this?"

"Who questioned you?"

Arkady reached into his coat pocket and withdrew two business cards. "Detective Hollins and Special Agent O'Shea." Arkady then added, "They seem to think the Old Man's death started the ball rolling for deaths of Yury and the newspaperman."

There were no reflective sunglasses to hide the eyes and facial expression of the brutish younger man standing across the table from him. The physical signals of a volcano about to erupt were plain to see. Arkady had pushed the right buttons, and now he was getting an answer to a question that had been bothering him for some time. With the disappearance of the accountant, he was even more suspicious. Vlad began cracking his neck from side to side, his neck muscles corded and the veins in his forehead throbbed. He stood straight up, threw his vacant chair skittering across the room and into the shins of one of his bodyguards.

Wide-eyed with spittle forming at the corner of his mouth, Vlad screamed, "You will report to me—" He lunged toward Arkady. "—any contact with the authorities." Throwing both palms in the middle of the table, placing his face directly across from Arkady's placid countenance, he hissed, "Is that clear?"

I have to get to that street bum before Vlad does, Arkady surmised nodding his head with a closed-eye wince. Does this asshole really have to spit on me?

CHAPTER EIGHTEEN

V lad was deep in thought when he departed the Old Man's house with his team. They took two executive protection black Chevy Suburbans and a car he was driving that they would leave behind. The across-town trip on this sunny, cloudless and unseasonably warm weekday was uneventful. He kept thinking about Arkady's surprise questions. His answer should have been, *What reporter?* But by acknowledging the reporter's death, he all but told Arkady that he had something to do with it.

The drive to West Philadelphia was uneventful. The GPS tracker on the target vehicle shows that it followed the same route that it had taken each of the past four days. Resupplying drug houses and picking up cash was a no-no, but this crew had gotten lazy and were doing both.

They were set up to intercept the van, make it look like a botched takedown and leave the rival gang's car at the scene with smoking automatic weapons still in it. Vlad's job was to take out the van driver then his crew would shoot up the van, leave the guns in the stolen car and take off in the Suburbans. The stolen car eased in front of the drug van from a parking spot and double parked. Vlad put on his mask and leaped out of the driver's seat with his automatic in hand. He put two rounds into the engine block and pointed his gun at the surprised driver of the van who crossed his arms across his face.

Just as he was about to squeeze off the fatal shots, he heard of his comms, "Get out! Get out! It's a trap."

An instant later, the sound of automatic weapons filled his eardrums. Vlad dropped and rolled under the drug courier's bulletproof van. Their protection was his momentarily. His team's warning saved his life. Could they suppress return fire long enough for him to get between the double-parked UPS and FedEx trucks?

A broad daylight takedown of a drug shipment was risky but was now made deadly by the chase car that the Jamaicans had never used before. Their back-up in that car was now crouched behind their armor-plated doors of the piece of shit sleeper car, and they were using their machine pistols with angry precision.

It would not take them long to lower their fire to under the van. When they went to reload, he sprinted to the gap between the delivery trucks and saw the FedEx driver crouched in the rear of his van behind some Amazon Prime boxes. Vlad leaped into the compartment with bullets whizzing by him and into the boxes lining the walls. He pointed his automatic at the driver and yelled, "Keys!"

Vlad's mask was firmly in place. The frightened driver reached into his pocket and threw them to Vlad. Vlad grabbed them and then the driver. Using him as a shield, they jumped out of the truck. He threw the driver into the bravest gunman exiting the courier's van. Vlad moved to the passenger side of FedEx van and then up into the driver's seat. The van's payload provided him protection from the barrage.

Having driven all types of vehicles in the former Soviet Bloc nations made it easy for him to bring the van to life. Grinding gears, he lurched into the intersection, where he made a quick right turn. He knew this vehicle had a GPS on it and it wouldn't be long before his position would be reported to the police. He scanned his mirrors. His team had kept the druggies pinned down. He was clear for now, but he had to ditch the van. If he could just make it to the Zoo.

Careening off of Girard Avenue, pedestrians in the crosswalks looked at the bounding brown truck with indignation, then terror as he barreled through their path, narrowly missing a woman with two young kids and a stroller. He banged on the horn as he approached the main entrance. Nothing was moving. He had to bail out. He hit the ground with his full-length suede leather coat shredding from the rough pavement while his Kevlar vest took the brunt of the impact. The van hit the ticket windows head-on with a sickening crunch. He rolled to a stop and ran thru traffic on 34th Street until he reached the embankment above the expressway and Martin Luther King Drive.

Scrambling down the hill and into a culvert gave him a minute to re-establish comms with his team. They had withdrawn according to their contingency plans without casualties. It wouldn't be long before the police would start searching for him with dogs. It was too risky for his team to try and make a pick-up. Could he carjack a motorist? Should he cross the Drive and drop into the river and let it carry him downstream? Just then a lone bicyclist appeared pedaling towards him. No cars were coming in either direction.

Four minutes later minutes, wearing a Cinzano bicycling form-fitting shirt above his slacks and dress shoes, Vlad crammed his head into the bike helmet and wobbled down the drive towards Center City and their rally point.

CHAPTER NINETEEN

Marsha had sat in the hot seat before. Across from her, on the upper floors of FBI offices, her supervisor was droning on about why she had to stand down on the Menke murder investigation. "Jingles," as the squad referred to him behind his back, earned that nickname from when, back in the day before cell phones and beepers, he would demand that agents check in with him regularly from pay phones. Subordinates had to keep pockets of loose change, lest they come up dry in the phone booth. The derisive nickname survived him into the digital age.

Darryl Stocker was ancient and would never rise to the level of Special Agent in Charge for the Eastern District of Pennsylvania's Philadelphia field office. As he got older and was repeatedly passed over for promotion, he added being a tight-ass desk jockey to his repertoire. It was said of this supervisory special agent that he never retreated, just that he backspaced a lot. An excellent investigation would never get an attaboy, and you better believe that he would go through your report with a red pen bequeathed to him from the nuns who taught fourth grade at Our Mother of Consolation to check your grammar and punctuation. God forbid that you would fail to scan in a receipt for a corresponding expense on your expense report. Jingles would hold it for a month or two and return it to you for correction.

She swore he got a chubby every time new guidelines were issued from D.C. He would pore over the orders the way her adolescent brother studied a *Penthouse* magazine. Most times, she could play the game, however this morning, she was in no mood.

"The guy was investigating the mob. He dies in the middle of the most bloodshed amongst the crime families since the '60s." Marsha said.

"You fail to understand that because of that exact reason, you cannot go off on your personal quest to solve the murder. The resources of your squad are stretched to the limit, and with the guidelines on overtime, there is no time to pursue this obtuse connection."

Obtuse connection, my ass. "Maybe it is me, I guess. Killing a reporter before they start reporting on organized crime, for which this squad thanks its existence to, looks like a priority to me. Today it's a reporter, tomorrow it's a private eye, the next day it's a—"

Jingles sighed a patronizing sigh. "Again you point out this is a murder. The last time I looked at this matter, Philadelphia Homicide was all over it, and their own OC unit backed away when Sullivan became a person of interest."

Marsha said, "They also are investigating the deaths of the three pedestrians at the Zoo that got killed when the hijacked FedEx van plowed into the main gate. The perp just escaped a shoot 'em up during a botched drug shipment and fled the scene. They are looking at that as a straight up street level homicide involving drugs, and that's it."

"And you think that those killings are related?" Jingles asked.

"No different than the three guys that get offed in front of the stash house. Military precision and automatic weapons. Same MO."

"That has yet to be proven—"

It was Marsha's turn to cut him off. "When Vasily Pavlichenko died, the whole shit storm started. The killings are part of the power vacuum caused by his death. My gut tells me that there is a guiding hand in this madness and that the reporter's death is smack dab in the middle of it."

"Yes, let's immediately spare two special agents right away because your gut says there's a grand conspiracy about an old man we haven't heard a peep from in about fifteen years."

"We stopped listening after 9-11 is the simple truth and that is the fact, Jack." Marsha was not budging.

"While your initiative in your assignments is commendable, O'Shea, you must remember that you are not assigned to investigate the death of Stewart Menke. I suggest you return to completing the link analysis of all the people who attended Pavlichenko's wake with all the organized crime related murders that have taken place since. That is where your time is best spent."

With that, she shook her head, uncrossed and stretched her legs, bolted to her feet and without another word, spun out of his office. The last time that guy had a gut feeling was when he was constipated.

"I don't get it, Marsh, you were a team player in high school and college, captain of the volleyball team. You sailed through Quantico near the top of your class in all the categories including shooting. You were a solid teammate back in your running and gunning days down in Miami. Now, you're this loner on some kind of quest. You gotta give it a rest. Your boss is telling you to stand down, your teammates are giving you the stink eye, my homicide people are telling me how cranky you've become."

Marsha and Nick were meeting for happy hour. She was chasing Irish coffees with a double espresso while he enjoyed a Corona with a lime.

"We've got this, okay? Once in a while, the Philly PD can actually solve a murder. Some of the latents that came back from the murder weapon will be the basis for Sullivan's arrest, but they want to make sure that they rule out other trace evidence that can't be explained."

"Like what?" Marsha asked.

"Like there are some other clothing fibers embedded in the bat that didn't come from what either Menke or Sullivan were wearing," Nick said.

"Like a Temple Sweatpants and warm up jacket?" she offered.

"Yeah. How'd ya know?"

"When he finally was coherent, and that pain in the ass doctor granted us time to see him, he told us that Menke had given him a surprise birthday present, and that when he left, he brushed up against a kid wearing Temple sportswear. And that Menke was very much alive. Minutes after he heard the news of Menke's death, he blurted out to an AA meeting that he was the last person to see him alive. When you're homeless and hitting rock bottom, you don't beat to death the only guy that treats you like a human being and who gives you a birthday present."

"I'm not the bad guy here. I say we got this, we got this. You want something to look at, try this: the boys from Brighton Beach want to expand into Boston and Philly. Their leadership wants to re-shuffle the deck."

Marsha considered this. The largest Russian crime groups had strongholds in LA and NYC. With Pavlichenko's passing, the East Coasters might want to claim the territory back. It made sense to have everything funnel to NYC in the vacuum that was created.

"Arkady Valnikov handles the waterfront for the Russians here. He was tight-lipped about his involvement in illegal activities, but he was concerned about the bloodshed. He can't deny the fact that he was at the Old Man's wake. I would have to guess that the killing at the gentlemen's club was to remove the Old Man's heir apparent and send a message to the remaining capos that they would have a new leader."

Nick said, "It fits your marching orders to work the OC angle, and you might tie the killings to a power move out of NYC."

Marsha mulled it over as she stirred some hot water into the dregs of her espresso. They returned to family and sports, notably how better the Sixers were doing in yet another rebuilding year.

When they left, she hugged her brother and thanked him for the lead. She started walking back to her office, and he yelled back to her.

"What was the present?"

"Dunno. Menke told him not to open it until his birthday, which he couldn't do because he was in the hospital."

Nick gave her a thumbs up that he understood and they went back to their separate paths. Marsha made her way along the slushy sidewalks that were icing up now that the sun was down.

Jingles should be gone by now, she thought. The squad room will be empty, save for Ramit, whom she promised a nice dinner for his extra time.

CHAPTER TWENTY

When did they position a policeman outside my door? Sully's hospital stay had been a rollercoaster of dreamy consciousness and medication-induced naps. The nurses were pumping him full of meds to counteract his alcohol poisoning and the doctor gave him something for anxiety.

During his times of lucidity, the doctor listened to him about the triggers that sent him into a blackout. Sully talked at length about his slide from returning decorated veteran to Listerine Man. The doctor was a good listener and a far cry from the emergency room docs that he dealt with on too many occasions over the past twenty-six months. This was the closest to death he had come since back in the Sandbox. Sully had been ready to start over and realized how he had no control over how he responded to Stew's horrible death.

"They put the cop out there this morning," the doctor said when he made his rounds. "*The Daily Sun*, quoting anonymous sources in the police department, says you're a 'person of interest' in the beating death of one of their reporters."

"I remember telling the cops that I was the last person to see Stew alive. What day was that? They all have blended together lately." He caught sight of an old mugshot as the headline of the paper. An older one, where he was utterly unshaved and unkempt, looking crazy-eyed and dangerous.

The doctor looked at his clipboard and said. "Two days ago."

Sully fingered the two business cards in his pocket.

Stew was alive when he left. He wasn't making that up. Semper Fi, Stew.

The doctor interrupted Sully's spiraling downward thoughts. "Mr. Sullivan, it's hard to think that anything can be worse than having your face splashed over the front page of a newspaper in an article about a grisly murder, but try to remember that you almost froze to death. What you have been dealing with, or more appropriately, what you haven't been treating for two years is the slow-motion death sentence of alcoholism and PTSD."

"Where do we go from here, Doc?"

"Antabuse will make you sick as a dog if you drink. Ten times worse than downing a bottle of mouthwash ever did. That's our deterrent. The good news is that your liver can handle it. Unfortunately, it doesn't play well with other meds and the best we can do is give you Ativan for the panic attacks, anxiety and stress of getting sober and dealing with your PTSD.

"I have scheduled for you to get out-patient help through the VA. They have an intake person coming over today to meet with you and go over the protocols."

"Why me, Doc?" Sully asked.

"Sully, no one really understands yet why alcohol and—"

"No", Sully interrupted, "Why are you doing this for me?"

The doctor took off his glasses and looked out at the snow coming down. "I didn't get to know my father. He had trouble adjusting to the real world when he came back from 'Nam. Um, he, he—"

"He was a marine?" Sully asked. The doctor nodded, put his

glasses back on, took a deep breath, stood up and squeezed Sully on the good shoulder and walked out.

Sully stared out the window at the fine mist of swirling snowflakes. It made him think of the blowing sand when he was wounded and later was awarded his Bronze Star. He was part of a two-man scout sniper team dropped off in the middle of Taliban country. They had been giving coordinates for air strikes for nearly two weeks with devastating effect.

Movement by the Taliban in that sector virtually ceased during their time out on their own.

After one devastating strike, the Taliban figured out they were being shadowed. Sully and his spotter Willie, from Wilmington, NC, called in for a hot extraction and broke cover just as they were almost stepped on.

Wille lifted his M-16 and sprayed the three fighters closest to them while Sully calmly tracked the leader, who was positioning troops from atop the ridge line and dropped him at four hundred yards. They began running to the opposite ridge line where the pickup was to take place. The CH-46 Sea Knight and two Super Cobra attack copters arrived just as they reached the bottom of the hill. Sully turned and saw Willie go down. The attack copters let loose with their 20mm M197 Gatling cannons in time to allow Sully to return to Willie and throw him over his shoulders. Sully ran like an option quarterback up the hill for 200 yards while the hunkered down Taliban fired back.

Sully wanted to stop when he felt like he couldn't keep running, but what choice did he have? He found the strength to push through the pain screaming out of his legs. Moving his legs faster than a walking pace, he couldn't stop. Stopping meant they're both dead. He set Willie down just as the Sea Knight's twin rotors bathed them in fine dust. The medics jumped out for Willie and dragged him the open bay door and Sully was lead, gasping for breath, inside after Willie was secured. With a whine of the rotors and an upward lurch they were airborne. The other medic crawled over to Sully after they stabilized Willie.

The medic cut back the Ghillie Suit, and Sully saw the blood dripping from the shreds the medic was removing. His through-and-through shoulder wound where he thought Willie had punched him began barking at him. That was the last part of the copter ride Sully remembered, before waking up in the field hospital.

CHAPTER TWENTY-ONE

"You have visitors," the nurse said.

"Shit. Cops again?" Sully asked.

"Surprise. It's your family."

"Shit. Shit."

"What's wrong?" she asked.

Sully glanced at his newspaper picture and at his reflection in the window. "They can't see me like this. Can you stall them for a minute?"

"Why?"

"I need a minute." Sully was determined not to let his family see the guy that he had become. Sure, he was getting stronger every day and the meds were starting to kick in, but was he strong enough to face them, especially looking like he did with his shipwreck beard and long hair? He drew a blank.

The nurse said, "Yeah. Let's see what we can do." She ducked behind the other side of a curtain and came back with a pair of scissors. A few dozen snips and clips here and there, and Listerine Man was gone.

A few minutes later, his daughter led the parade into his room. He had left the family when she was two and a half and now she was almost five. Brittany was beautiful, all bundled up in her long coat and snow boots. She pulled off her bunny ears hat and her long chestnut blonde hair fell to her shoulders. At first she was hesitant, not knowing how to act, but then she rushed to his arms. "Hi, Daddy."

Sully breathed her into his embrace and closed his eyes tight. He opened his eyes to see his estranged wife Tricia standing behind his daughter, biting her lip. It was safe here, they knew it. Nothing bad was going to happen today. His father Joseph Sr., mother and brother filled out the back row. Each carried a bag.

"Daddy, I made this card for you." Brittany handed him her drawing of rainbows, unicorns, and horses under a blue sky. In the middle of it, the three of them were holding hands.

"How much snow did you guys get from the storm?" Sully asked his dad.

"Little over two feet, but it drifted."

His mom piped in, "You know your father, he couldn't wait. He cleared out our driveway and Old Mrs. Chalmer's."

"Roads bad?"

His younger brother Bill answered, "95 was okay but the roads getting over here were a little sketchy. Glad I had the four-by."

Each took turns presenting their gifts: a multi-purpose tool from his brother, thermal underwear from his mother, and Phillies tickets for the opener against the Nationals from his father. Somehow, father and son could always put aside their differences and talk baseball for nine innings. It was an olive branch for sure.

But the best present of all was Tricia sitting there smiling and not crying.

He knew he was a long way from reuniting. Spare bedrooms in three houses were offered and declined. Sully had to get sober, stay sober and get treated for an elephant in the room that today seemed a little less looming. He would earn the right to a roof over his head, a lock on his door, a warm bed, a refrigerator to peer into and long hot showers. He would come home with his father right from the ballgame.

After the final hugs from his daughter and mother followed by arm punches from the men, Tricia was now seated next to his bed, and they were alone. He noticed she was still wearing her ring.

"She's growing like a weed. She wasn't that tall when I left."

"Brittany knows that you had to leave to get better. We pray for you every night before I read her bedtime stories. Seeing you in the hospital lets her think that you've been sick all this time."

Sully agreed with the explanation to a toddler. It was better than telling her that he was a monster. "I have to wait until a spot opens up in the half-way house next to the VA. They've got programs and my medication plan in place. All Saints has an AA meeting every evening."

"This should make it a little easier to get back and forth." She handed him a monthly bus and subway pass from SEPTA. Briefly, their fingers touched on the handoff. Then their eyes connected. She leaned forward and kissed him on the cheek, and he reached out with both arms and embraced her for what felt like their first time back in High School. Wet-eyed and sniffling back her emotions, she stood and said, "Don't ever cut your own hair again."

He laughed. "This one was all nurse, I swear."

After his family disappeared down the hall, Sully was left with his thoughts. He didn't have all the answers, but he had a goal. He knew that he may get arrested at any moment for a crime he didn't commit, but he had to keep moving forward. But how?

The doctor and the man from Security interrupted his contemplations.

"Mr. Sullivan, you have to sign for all your stuff that you were wearing and carrying when they found you."

Sully glanced at his parka, snow pants, combat boots, and

backpack and scribbled his name on the sheet. The man shifted back and forth on balls of his feet until the doctor said, "We got it from here, Murph."

He wasn't bashful in front of the doctor as he put on the thermals then the rest of the clothes. He found a pocket for the all-in-one tool and the ball tickets in his pants. He left the sweatshirt on the bed. He refused the wheelchair giving the wheelchair attendant a nod. It was time to go.

"It's simple, Sully, you drink, and you die." the doctor said, "Your family still loves you. You've got a lot to live for."

Sully nodded.

"Semper Fi, Sully."

"Semper Fi, Doc."

Outside, he took a deep breath of the frigid February air. It had been a mild winter so far, but now Old Man Winter was letting the Delaware Valley know who was boss. Sully got his bearings and began walking toward F Troop. Is my tent still there? It was a premium space on the dry, sheltered-from-the-wind loading dock. He was lost in thought of how he had gotten to this place as he made his way in the streets as many of the sidewalks in front of vacant industrial building were not shoveled.

He passed two garbage dumpsters in the bright sunshine before plunging into the relative darkness under the bridge.

He heard the voice first from behind. "Turn 'em out."

He spun around and was face to face with a white guy who looked a lot worse for wear than himself. The guy was back-lit, and Sully's eyes had trouble adjusting. This is why the guy picked this place. Sully fixated on the long and gleaming serrated hunting blade that could gut him like a deer.

Sully knew two things immediately. What he had was not worth fighting for and that he wasn't ready for a fight. This guy was desperate. Sully slowly lowered his backpack to the ground and very slowly reached for his right wrist and said, "I just got released from Detox." Pointing to his wristband. "This is all I have." He nudged the backpack towards his assailant.

Looking down at the backpack and up at Sully, he said, "The coat, too. Leave it, then turn around and run."

Sully began backing away while unzipping his parka and dropped it to the ground, then took off running. *Just my luck that I'd have to be the same size as that guy.* Sully lamented as the icy cold air blasted him.

Sully sprinted to the other side of trestle and turned around to see the parka and backpack hopping and bopping in the opposite direction. He was safe. He kept jogging, but instead of heading towards F Troop, he changed course away from the River and back towards Temple University. He jogged slowly to the Unitarian Church. He would retrieve the gifts given to him by Stew.

The robber had indeed run in the opposite direction and zig-zagged through cleared streets and snow-clogged alleys. He stopped behind a bodega on Kensington Avenue. He began rummaging through the backpack. His back was to the street when he heard footsteps behind him.

He whirled to see a man wearing a long leather jacket. On the man's waist was a police badge. He thought twice about reaching for his knife that he had set down next to his bounty. He slowly stood up and put his hands away from his body. "Boy, you guys work fast, you got me." His bearded face was still partially shrouded by the parka.

The plainclothes officer reached for the blade and turned it over in his left hand, feeling both its heft and balance. "Sure do." Came the reply with an upward thrust into the man's stomach. With his right hand, he covered the robber's mouth and pivoted the robber against the side of the building. The cop angled the hunting knife up through the robber's stomach and into his heart.

The spurting, pulsing blood saturated the inside of the zipped-up parka.

The robber was eyeball to eyeball with his killer when his life ended. The policeman took out the blade, dropping the lifeless body to the ground, saw that he had no blood spatter on his clothes or shoes and retrieved the GPS unit that Director of Hospital Security Murphy had secreted in the backpack.

CHAPTER TWENTY-TWO

Arkady Valnikov was alone and stood in the Old Man's basement. His bodyguard was working on an assignment for Vladislav. He never believed for a minute the accountant was on the beach in Belize, sipping Pina Coladas from a coconut shell delivered to him by a pretty brown-eyed girl.

This is where it happened.

The perfect outline of where a rug sat on the wood floor was made clear by the square of polished dust-free wood in the middle of the floor. That rug covered a trap door that Arkady lifted easily. Below it was a space carved out of the foundation for the floor safe. It was empty.

He turned and walked the perimeter of the basement. The casement window facing the sidewalk was dusty, filled with cobwebs and the remains of unlucky bugs. Pale washed out light fell in from the street. A single bulb attached to string offered the remaining light. The oil furnace, oil tank and hot water heater sat in one corner next to the old-fashioned fuse box.

Against the wall below the front entrance and sitting parlor were bedsheet-covered couches and a wooden serving table. The table had a fresh coat of dust on it. On either side of the table, Arkady could see where the sheet that had been draped over it ended and a thicker layer of dust began on the upholstered chairs. The sheet and the rug are gone. One to wipe up the blood and the other to carry the body out.

Arkady walked to the shared wall with the row home to the left and found a simple workbench. The vise bolted on one front edge was rusted closed. Across the table were scattered various plumbing and electric tools from a by-gone era. The pegboard behind it still held simple hand tools for minor home repairs. Was it missing? He looked on the shelf below he couldn't find it. He went upstairs and walked around each room and opened drawers and closets and came back to the basement. No hammer. That's what Vlad tortured him with.

To be sure, Arkady swept the flashlight beam under the tables. He was about to shut it off when he saw something reflecting light below the serving table. The accountant's glasses! They were unmistakable. They came off during the torture or when Bad Vlad hefted him up in the rolled-up carpet as he carried him out.

Fibers from the carpet were snagged to the unpainted rough-hewn wood frame at the top of the stairs where Vlad had to make a ninety-degree left turn. Again, more dust was brushed aside at shoulder level on the front door frame and on the screen door as it would have closed behind Vlad and the carpet over his right shoulder on the way out. Cambria led to C Street. A left would take towards many derelict industrial lots where a body could be dumped, and a right would take him to the river. Where could Bad Vlad back up his Chevy Suburban and push the body into the river?

Arkady knew the Waterfront. He knew where the Old Man made problems disappear. He had been to that spot years ago, when he helped the Old Man deposit an informant, about to testify against them, into the chilly Delaware. The Old Man would have shown Bad Vlad this spot.

The ramshackle three-story concrete building was still there. Open on both ends, Arkady saw tire tracks from the mud leaving prints on the concrete leading to the inlet. Under cover of the building, a concrete U-shaped cut out allowed for a medium sized barge to be loaded from three sides where the tugboat would back it out and push it downstream.

The rug or sheet left no trace. If the body were weighted down too heavily, it would be sitting there at the bottom of the cut-out. If it became buoyant, it might snag along the rotting piers and jetties north of Penn's Landing. The trick was to help it out to the current downstream.

Arkady walked the length of the cut out to the river. Nothing there. Dress shoes slick from soft semi-frozen mud made slippery footing along the Philly shoreline until it became impossible to traverse swampy land reclaimed by the river and long since abandoned by those hoping to make their living legitimately on the waterfront. The Old Man taught him well.

Arkady was convinced this was how the accountant met his fate. But why? Why did the accountant have to die? How was he a threat to Vlad? What did the accountant know? The man lived like a pauper.

From the body drop to the accountant's apartment was just a short drive.

Arkady entered the vestibule and saw junk mail spilling from his mailbox to the floor. They would just keep delivering it because that's what they do. The third-floor apartment had a flimsy lock on the door. With one finger, he was able to push the old door in. Someone had shouldered their way into his apartment exploding the lock from the door jam. The three rooms were professionally tossed. The contents of the freezer were on the floor to the delight of scurrying cockroaches and millipedes. Drawers were emptied and lay like dead soldiers. The few worn pots and pans were dumped into the sink. The accountant's bed and dresser were upended, and his few possessions were violently scattered about.

In the small living room, cushions from his living room couch were knifed open, and the stuffing spilled out on the floor. A saucer and empty teacup sat undisturbed on the end table below the reading lamp. A used tea bag rested in a recycled pudding cup on top of a folded newspaper. He opened it up to see *The Daily Sun* column of Stew Menke. The tumblers in his mind quickly fell into place. The accountant knew something and gave it to the reporter. The visit from the authorities now made much more sense. The Old Man, the accountant, and the reporter all died at the hand of one man.

Back to the waterfront. He knew precisely where the encampment was. Daylight was turning to dusk when a man stepped in front of him.

"Can I help you?" It was more a challenge than a question.

"I am looking for Mr. Sullivan," Arkady replied pleasantly.

"You a cop?"

"No, I have a freight transfer business, not far from here. I was hoping to speak with him on a private matter."

"Sully is a popular guy lately."

"How so, if I may ask?" Arkady asked with politeness borne out of genuine curiosity.

Checkpoint Charlie looked at Arkady's business card and at Arkady. "Seems like a lot of people are looking for him. Cops were here a couple of times and went through his tent. I asked them if they had a warrant and they told me that they didn't need no stinkin' warrant. Then there were the bikers. Mean dudes. They respected my time in the army but said they have business with Sully too. Then the commotion died down, and nobody's been asking for him for about a week now."

"Hey, Charlie, What's up?"

Both men turned to look at Joseph Sullivan wearing an insulated dress raincoat, slacks, dress shoes and Kangol cap.

CHAPTER TWENTY-THREE

Both men were drinking instant coffee made from the boiling water in the pot on Sully's sterno rig. It also served to warm the tent where the two reasonably well-dressed men sat cross-legged. Sully could tell by the look on Arkady's face that the math didn't add up.

"You're wondering why I'm dressed so nice. The church where I keep my belongings had a clothing drive, and seeing how I was robbed Friday, I was going to be very cold," Sully said, then added, "I don't get to dress up anymore."

"You were robbed?"

"I wasn't out of the hospital for more than 30 minutes, and a guy jumped me and said he would filet me like a fish unless I gave him my backpack and heavy coat."

"I'm sorry to hear that. Were you hurt?"

"No. He would have stuck me like a pig if I didn't give him what he wanted. He had crazy eyes. How can I help you Mr. VAL NI KOV?" Sully read phonetically from Arkady's business card.

"You said you were in the hospital."

"After I heard that my friend Stew died, I drank myself into a blackout and almost froze to death. The hospital got me straightened out. I spent nearly a week there."

Arkady took this in and placed his cup on the ground cover. "Your coffee is horrible, Mr. Sullivan, but I appreciate your hospitality without knowing who I am or what I want. You were probably safe while you were in the hospital. I have come to tell you that I think you are in danger."

"Why's that?"

"We both have been interviewed by the authorities in the death of your friend Stewart Menke."

"I'm listening."

"Mr. Menke was going to start writing about organized crime in Philadelphia. I believe he was killed because he knew something."

"Mr. Valnikov, I suspected that much myself. Stew was acting strangely in the week before he was killed. He said it was big, but he wouldn't tell me anything. I told the cops all this. Why did they question you?"

"My long-time employer died less than a month ago. He was in the business that Mr. Menke was going to expose. My employer's accountant went missing a short time later after your friend died. He kept the books and knew the secrets. He also had kept the article that your friend wrote on his reading table. I do not believe that these deaths and the explosion of violence in my world are by chance or coincidence."

"Your employer? Your world? Stew and I talked about all the shootings and bombings like it was the Wild West. Are you saying that you are connected to all this?" Sully asked.

"Not the killings. My business depends on greased palms and people looking the other way. I don't think you need to know more about how it all works, but I could not approach you with some nonsense. You would see right through me."

"You tell me that I am in danger and you tell me that you are in the business that Stew was going to write about yet you come to warn me instead. I don't get it," Sully said, reaching into his birthday present bag and pulling out a bag of cookies. "Care for some?"

"Normally, I would politely decline, but I famished."

Somehow eating cookies in a tent and thinking about what was going to be said next didn't need to be rushed. The two men were forming a simple bond from sharing food while they warmed themselves by a fire.

Sully wasn't sure if this man was ever in the Service or the Russian version of the Boy Scouts. He didn't look like an outdoorsy type at all, with his finely tailored clothes and awfully muddy soft-leather shoes.

Arkady was first to speak. "They are addicting. Thank you, but no more for now. Mr. Sullivan, my motives are very simple, and you may not like to hear them, but you may see the wisdom of my warning to you. The killer knows that you were the last person to see your friend alive. The killer probably didn't get what he was looking for, given how badly your friend was tortured before he died. The killer had to assume that your friend told you what he knew. He has to silence you before you can expose him."

"As I told you and the cops, Stew didn't tell me anything. He was on to something, but I don't know what. He was scared with good reason."

"He died protecting a secret. If he made arrangements for what he knew to be made public, it would have come out by now. He died a violent death rather than give his killer what he wanted. Since the killer didn't get what he wanted from your friend, he cannot take a chance that you know something."

Sully began thinking about his present situation. If this was true, he could not stay here. He couldn't go to be with family and bring danger to them. Going to the halfway house or VA hospital was out of the question, he would be a sitting duck. His plans to get sober and treated for PTSD were like clouds racing to the horizon.

"It is not a good situation, I agree, Mr. Sullivan. If the killer doesn't get to you first, the police may have you arrested for your friend's murder. You wouldn't last long in prison waiting for your trial, I'm afraid."

"I can't go to the cops. They are going to say that I made up this story to throw the spotlight away from me."

"You have another option, Mr. Sullivan."

CHAPTER TWENTY-FOUR

"What happened?" Vlad asked his source.

"Sullivan left the hospital with the GPS in the backpack, the GPS was working perfectly. When he was discharged, he was wearing a blue parka that went down to his knees. That is the description I got."

"But you tell me the dead man who was found behind the store was a common thief, a low-life junkie who was wearing the parka and had the backpack."

"When I came up from behind him, his face was partially shrouded by the hood of the parka. It was freezing cold. The guy looked just like the mugshot I had for him." The source avoided saying what happened next.

Vlad shook his head. "Amateur."

"Really? The information I gave you on the drug shipment was good, but they surprised you and innocent people in my town died because your plans didn't take into account that they had a follow vehicle full of guys with machine guns. You are lucky to be alive. This is a very deadly game you are playing."

He continued, "I made a mistake. Sullivan was robbed under the train tracks probably where I lost the visual on him. What were the chances of that happening? He's one lucky bastard. He didn't die in the freezing cold, and he didn't die behind the store."

Vlad countered with a quiet, steady voice and jabbing finger. "Worse, you tell me this dead man had multiple IDs on him, and it took the weekend for his prints to identify him. Who attended the autopsy?"

The source spit back, "I didn't think I had to look at him twice. I was confident that they would identify Sullivan. I was wrong."

"Where is our reporter's friend now?" Vlad fumed.

"He's back at his tent. As soon as I found out we had the wrong guy, I had a car go by there. We haven't lost him."

"I will deal with this man myself," Vlad said.

"Why? It doesn't seem like he has said anything to anybody."

Vlad shook his head. "The bum was admitted to the hospital in a blackout. He doesn't remember anything from the time he learned of the reporter's death until they revived him. What is not to say that he will regain his memory at some later time? What if he remembers what the reporter told him? What if he remembers seeing me and can describe me as the student that was walking into the apartment building when he was walking out? No. He is a loose end that must be cut off."

Valnikov rubbed the circulation back into his knees, stood up and shook Sully's hand before exiting the encampment. He left Sully to consider his proposal. Sully had his suspicions about this Russian's motives and wasn't trusting his own instincts to read this man either. In his two-plus years on the street, he had been burned a few times by good-time drinking buddies and supposed friends. He reached into the bag given to him by Stew the night that Stew died. He ripped off the birthday paper haphazardly covering a square cardboard box. Nestled inside tissue was a signed baseball. It was from all the players on the 1980 World Champion Philadelphia Phillies. Sully turned it over in his hand and could make out many of the signatures. Stew had written on a simple plain white invitation.

Sully

Semper Fi

Stew

Sully gripped the ball and cried, muffling his sobs so his neighbors wouldn't hear. He hadn't sincerely mourned his friend, or maybe more correctly, didn't remember mourning his friend. For a couple years, he was drowning his emotions in the bottle and numbing all feelings. He was very alive and feeling emotional pain for the first time in a very long time. It hurt. It all hurt.

He wanted to let Stew know that he could be strong now. He gingerly wrapped the ball back in the tissue and placed the card and the ball back in the box. He placed it in the bag Stew gave him, and that is when he noticed the second box at the bottom of the bag.

CHAPTER TWENTY-FIVE

The swamp was bone cold and wet. He had done his basic in the summer at Parris Island, then advanced courses in both Georgia and North Carolina where he honed his craft as a Scout Sniper. Wet was part of the 24-hour, 7 days a week ordeal of that summer and fall of 2002, but it wasn't both this wet and cold. Two tours in Afghanistan had been skin-cracking dry in both temperature ranges. Today, though his new winter fatigues were warm and dry, his teeth still chattered and his eyes watered. Damned cold.

His ground cloth was water-resistant and radiated his own body heat back up to his prone body, but the wind on his back wicked away the warmth. The combat boots were new and fit snugly over his two layers of socks. The ground cover matched the surplus store outfitting. Both sets of binoculars gave him no light, low light, and daylight magnification. From this vantage point, he was far enough away to see F Troop in its entirety and his tent with the two surprises in it.

Doc had met him in the parking lot of the hospital after they talked on the phone and he re-supplied Sully with the meds he would need until this op was completed. It went without saying that Sully couldn't go to the cops with his new information. They would say that after Sully beat Stew to death, he ransacked the house looking for money and ended up taking what was in his bag.

Somehow, the focus of his mission made the need for alcohol less pressing; the situational anxiety sublimated by the steady dose of focus. He was calm in his element. This is what he was good at. This is what he was trained to do. He was battle-tested in the real sense of the word. He had been wounded in battle. He had seen death all around him.

This was not a foreign country, but his own turf. His mission was to find out who killed Stew, and to determine if they were coming after him. He had snuck out of F Troop catching up with Valnikov within minutes of discovering the second box in his bag. He returned before dawn with his goodies. The sun rose from behind him the next morning, and before anyone stirred, he had finished the last touches on his sniper hide. Snipers took great pride and care in hiding. Their lives depended on it.

To the casual observer, two hundred yards away, nothing was amiss. He had to blend in with the landscape and vegetation. To the trained seeker, only his binos would leave a reflection. He broke enough shards of glass and tilted them in a similar angle to both sides and front and back of his spot to confuse the seeker. He had given a passing thought to bringing a rifle, as this job only required observation and that is how he drew up his action plan.

Valnikov made his proposal very clear; If you want to hunt a Siberian tiger, you could go out in the harsh landscape and try to stalk the beast. You follow tracks, you sit upwind. You eat vegetarian with no spices, so your sweat doesn't give off any clues. You study droppings. On the other hand, you could tie up a goat to a post with a bell around its neck and wait for the predator to get hungry. That is what they agreed to do.

The dawn brought clear blue skies and a stiff breeze from the west into his face. Some campers woke up early and queued for the shower. Then the second wave stirred. Sully knew many of the campers, but none of them stopped at his tent to check on him. The silhouette, backlit by the rising sun, in his tent was pretty clear even without magnification. Throughout the day, vets came and went. No one paid much attention to Sully's tent. He watched and waited. Some days it was like that. Hours passed, and shadows moved.

The night light in the tent turned on shortly after dusk and illuminated the inside of his tent. The snow started with the drop in temperature and an uptick on the wind. Flurries at first and as sunset became twilight, the snow started coming down heavier. The wind whistled over his head. His tent was a faint soft light in the swirling snow as nightfall took hold. His new cell phone's weather app had said that this storm that would dump another 12-15 inches before ending at daybreak. Visibility was miserable. The snowstorm would also muffle any sounds of footsteps.

His plan wasn't so great now, he realized. Should he try to venture closer and burrow into snow drifts directly across from the dock? Would his approach be seen by anybody watching? His quarry could be savvy and be employing counter-surveillance as he pondered this dilemma.

At 3 a.m., he saw a shape, then lost it in the snow and glimpsed it again. Something was moving towards his tent with speed and stealth. Then it disappeared again. The binoculars only made it worse as snowflakes seemed as large as the ones that festooned Market Street in front of the Old Gallery when he was a kid coming downtown at Christmas time. Two football fields away in a blizzard under cover of darkness, he lay there with only one hope now.

Suddenly, the dock exploded in white light and Chinese firecrackers. He saw the white-clad man built like a fullback tear out of the tent at full speed. The man ran first in the direction from where he came and then veered back towards Sully. He was backlit by the firestorm that now engulfed the tent. Sully didn't have time to mourn the loss of the toy store man-sized Winnie the Pooh. The stuffed-animal killer was headed right towards him, and all Sully had was his all-in-one tool. The blade was four inches long, but as a wise man once said, don't bring a knife to a gun fight.

He stayed still. Sully's would-be attacker had the advantage of the light behind him now showing him where to run in the swamp. He lurched to a stop ten feet in front of Sully with his chest heaving. Sully could see his nostrils fogging the air through his ski-mask. At best, Sully could hope to stab him in the leg and sever an artery, but that wouldn't slow down a bullet from the automatic with a silencer. With his other hand, the man pulled out his cell phone and took off his right glove to press the screen.

Pooh's executioner spoke rapidly in an Eastern European language that Sully didn't understand. The conversation went back and forth briefly, and then with a new bearing, the steroid ninja was off running again, but not before tossing the cell phone into the snow drift next to Sully's head.

Sully watched F Troop come alive. Some firecrackers were still going off, some were smoldering, and the smell of gunpowder wafted towards him in waves. His tent was a bonfire and lit up the dock. Some of the veterans tried beating down the flames with wet blankets once the fireworks subsided. Sully reached over to the phone, and using his fingers like a pair of pliers, delicately deposited it into a used baggie.

Next time he would bring a gun to a gun fight.

Things quieted down after the fire department came and hit the entire area around his tent with a water cannon. Then the police arrived. First the uniforms, then later he spotted plain-clothesmen through his binoculars.

One well-dressed male, acting like a superior officer in a long black leather coat, seemed most interested in the scene and remained long after the others departed. Sully could make out his features and wondered why the man needed to kick the now-charred and crispy Pooh bear.

Before dawn, when all was quiet, he stood up, stuffed his ground cloth in his backpack, collected his kit bag and walked to the designated pick-up. The snow had stopped, and his footsteps were quiet on drifted over streets. This section of town was not high on the plow routes. No city councilpersons lived around F Troop.

The sleek Mercedes SUV pulled up, and he got in. It pulled away sluggishly and slip-slided along unto better roads that had gotten a once over with plow blade.

"You were right, They tried to come after me." Sully said.

"How many?" the driver asked.

"Just one."

"What did he look like?"

"Just under six foot. Two hundred. Solid. Wearing all white." Sully related the story of how when the attacker took on Winnie The Pooh, he tripped the wire that set off the firecrackers purchased for a premium in Chinatown the night before.

"What else?"

"Speak to me in Russian," Sully said.

"What?"

"Speak to me in Russian."

"What should I say?" Arkady asked.

"Tell me what you had to eat today, I don't care. Anything." Sully said.

So Arkady did, and after he finished, Sully said, "Yeah, he sounds like you. Can we stop at a diner?"

Arkady said, "Come with me to my home. I will make you breakfast, Mr. Sullivan."

"Call me Sully. That's what my friends call me."

"Sully, is there anything else?"

"Put that guy in a Temple tracksuit and take off the mask and I'd bet my bottom dollar that he was the one that brushed past me as I walked out of Stew's apartment building. My memory is still sketchy, so I'm not 100% positive."

"I think I know who he is."

Sully remained silent.

Arkady continued, "If he is who I think he is, his name is Vladislav Balderis. He was my employer's enforcer until he hastened my employer's death."

Arkady replayed the hospital scene as if it was yesterday. They were riding on Roosevelt Boulevard heading to the western suburbs. The road was slow but passable. Philadelphia was waking up with the sun chasing the lingering storm clouds away.

Sully retrieved the baggie from his kit bag with the cell phone. "Is there a way to get his fingerprints?"

"This is interesting. Where did you find it?"

"He tossed it after he finished speaking in Russian and took off. He wasn't more than ten feet away from me and almost hit me in the head when he threw it away," Sully said.

"It's a burner phone. He didn't want anybody to connect his regular phone with this attempt on your life."

Their conversation continued for some time until Sully's exhaustion took over. He hadn't slept since his hospital discharge.

Sully was just nodding off when Arkady turned up the local 24-hours news station and was jolted awake when he heard his name. The reporter explained how the police arrived just minutes after Sully's tent caught fire. They were on their way to serve an arrest warrant for the murder of Stew Menke.

That's why Mr. Trenchcoat was so pissed.

CHAPTER TWENTY-SIX

Somebody is pressuring Jingles to ride me like a drugstore pony, Marsha thought. Status updates on status updates were getting a bit tiresome. He closed his workday getting the last update with his coat and hat on before heading out for hearth and home. Her day was only beginning.

Fueling up on blonde espressos and Chinese takeout, she sat side by side with Ramit in front of the whiteboard. With chopsticks in hand above the carton just below her chin, she watched as he added the latest intel to the board.

"The shell casings from failed drug shipment robbery near the Zoo matched those found later at drive-by outside the motorcycle gang's clubhouse killing two. Both dead bikers were the muscle for the Harbison Ave. Sports Bar and Grille. It's a connection back to the Russians again," Ramit said.

"The shooters knew we would make the connection." She studied the board and asked, "Why?"

Ramit stared at the puzzle. "It's saying the shooters are going after both the Jamaicans and the Russians."

"Unless, it is part of the misdirection with the killing of the Russian and the Jamaicans that got pinned on the South Philly guy which touched off the whole shooting war in the first place," she countered.

Sandwiched between those two similar events, the carnage on the whiteboard was more than the city had ever seen for such a short period. Adding to it, innocent people were getting mowed down by gunfire, explosions and runaway getaway vehicles.

The only name in black was still on the board. "Anything new on the Menke killing, Marsha?" Ramit asked.

She had argued with Jingles about keeping Menke's murder on the board, even after the word came down that a warrant went out on Sullivan.

"Hollins told me that the fibers on the bat and those transferred to Menke came from a Temple tracksuit sold at a dozen outlets around the university. The reporter's work computer and phone didn't have any more leads on it. His notebook appeared to have been written in his own crypto-shorthand, it is no longer being analyzed. Plus, now that Sullivan is a fugitive, it really points the finger at him."

"What do you think, Marsha?"

"Just so we are on the same page, Ramit, I haven't shared this with anyone. This is what has been keeping me up at night." She played Menke's voice message.

They listened in silence. Stew Menke's voice came on. They heard the strain in the older man's words, the pause and then the addendum. She played it again and stood up next to the board. "That's why he is up there on the board. I'm still kicking myself for just thinking Menke was another nosey reporter looking for a quote. I can't bring myself to tell Jingles I deleted the message without having listened to it all the way through."

"You met Mr. Sullivan. What do you think?"

Marsha thought carefully before answering. "He was coming off a major league bender. His blackout was very real. There's no doubting that. Did he kill Menke and then nearly drink himself to death? It's possible but unlikely. I think he saw the newscast just like he told the AA meeting, which we confirmed and then decided to get pickled."

"What about the man in the Temple tracksuit?"

"Still a sore spot with me, Ramit. The fibers from the tracksuit were embedded into the bat and into Menke's wounds. This was not a casual transfer on clothing. Sullivan admitted to handling the bat. It was a special gift from Joe DiNatale to Stew Menke when Menke was Phillies beat writer. Sullivan was a regular visitor to Menke's apartment according to neighbors. None of the fibers from his clothing were found on the bat or in Menke's wounds. But because they had Sullivan's fingerprints on the murder weapon, PD thought that was enough. A double win for Homicide. They clear the murder with an easy arrest when Sullivan surfaces."

"You didn't answer my question."

"No, I guess I didn't answer your question. The answer is I don't know what they did other than their lab doing matches exactly on the type of clothing that Sullivan described as to what the kid was wearing when he walked in while Sullivan was walking out the last time he saw Menke alive."

"Then the tracksuit was part of the disguise, no one would think twice of a young man wearing a Temple tracksuit within a short radius of the campus," he said.

"Go on," she said.

"He bought the tracksuit to kill Menke, and most likely, he didn't buy it online."

She put down her container of General Tso's chicken and handed him her fortune cookie. "We still have time to visit the University Bookstore, campus stores and licensees in the area to see if we can pull their video."

He got up to get his coat, and she stopped him. "What's it say?"

"What?" he replied.

"Your fortune cookie."

Ramit opened up the cellophane wrapper cracked open the cookie and read it to himself first and blushed deeply. "It's nothing really." He threw it away.

She fished it out of the trash can while he was getting his coat. She read: *A very attractive person has a message for you.*

They entered the elevator, and she pressed the button to go down to the garage.

CHAPTER TWENTY-SEVEN

The Rebel RPG struck the Georgian Military KrAZ-632 Transport truck on the driver's side door blowing Vlad out the passenger side door, just as machine gun fire raked its bed, killing or wounding many of the regular army passengers. The gas tank and extra munitions exploded in a deadly two-step frying everyone still on board. The burning metal from the twisted hulk rained down on him as he crawled into a ditch. The ditch was nothing more than a fat truck tire width of a rut, but he flipped onto his back in the brackish water, putting out the fire spreading across the back of his uniform and allowing him to escape the murderous ambush.

He had to submerge to where only his nose was above water while the rebels slaughtered the rest of the survivors that had scrambled out alive. His wounds did eventually heal, but they left a jagged quilt of grafts and scars across his shoulder blades.

He thought about this battle as he gently removed the gauze, lest it snagged on the part of his raw and ravaged skin. The aloe lotion was helping with the burns, but he was still angry about the ambush. Angry he had underestimated his foe and angry at Sullivan for lighting him up in a fireworks show. His winter camouflage outerwear had taken most of the brunt of the burning firecrackers, but some had penetrated the thin layers underneath. He was slowly removing the field dressings he received upon his extraction from the scene.

His right forearm had shielded his face and took the most damage, the burns were deepest there. His armpit was raw from the blisters, but they were starting to slowly heal. His pain was throbbing and incessant.

Sleep was out of the question, as he had a full day of collections and payments. The operation to eliminate Sullivan was rushed, and he cursed that he didn't have time to put the encampment under surveillance. A couple of days with two hidden cameras would have told him everything he needed to know about his adversary's movements. Instead, his source told him that the police were going to execute the arrest warrant in less than 4 hours, during the middle of the snowstorm.

He didn't want Sullivan making any deals with the police. Relying again on intel from the police source almost got him killed. First the drug shipment and now this. Vlad was angry at everybody. Sullivan made it clear with the booby-traps he had what Vlad wanted. He had the evidence the reporter had received from the accountant, and those things had gotten them killed.

Life in jail was a death sentence that Vlad feared, but not as much as all the other mob groups getting a chance to torture him to death if they got to him first. That is what kept him in Philadelphia. He had to eliminate his threat. No one had connected him yet to the mob hits that had turned the city into a war zone. If Sullivan released the video, Vlad would be safe nowhere and would have to go into hiding deep in the mountains. Fresh air and plenty of big game, yes, but it would be a very solitary life, and he could never lay his head down without worrying if he would wake up in the morning. All in all, his plan to upset the status quo between the crime families in town was working better than expected. Retribution killings were taking on a life of their own. Even fringe groups got bold enough to make a turf grab, mostly for meth and prostitution.

It was in this chaos that Vlad planned to offer his skills to each of the dominant groups to restore order. He and his enforcers would take a cut of every group's profits. The model was working with his Russian comrades, and he could prove his concept to the players that he had been playing very shortly. Each group would be weakened considerably and therefore be more willing for his assistance. He had to chuckle. He was taking a play from Old Man's playbook. All he had to do was create the environment for the groups to come to him.

Once the video surfaced, Vlad would have to start running for his life. Sitting there in a motel parking lot, he paid cash at the desk for the no questions asked hourly rate. He watched the giant claw machine across the road pick up junked cars and drop them into the crusher.

His pain fed his anger, and his anger fed his pain. Sleep was out of the question. Only one thing would bring him relief. Sullivan had to die. He watched another car disappear into the crusher.

CHAPTER TWENTY-EIGHT

"What are you telling me, Valnikov?" Hollins demanded. They sat in the back area of a Greek diner in Neshaminy up in Bucks County northeast of the city limits. Both ordered coffee and toasted corn muffins. The changing shift from breakfast to lunch was not paying them much attention. It was bright and sunny but was still achingly cold as the Canadian high swept down across the northeast.

"If my people knew I was meeting you, I would be dead by nightfall and never found again," Arkady replied. His bodyguard was otherwise occupied with Vlad again. Arkady had taken his Mercedes SUV to the gym and completely changed his clothes. He walked next door to the car rental agency and chose a nondescript SUV with tints. He now sat across from Hollins wearing his work out gear. He couldn't be too careful with a GPS or bug being placed on his car or sown into his coat. Actually, the other leaders of the Russian group would be in agreement that Vlad needed to be stopped. "What is going on is horrible. Nobody wants all this killing, especially of civilians."

"Thank you for saying that, Valnikov. I'm genuinely touched." Hollins smirked.

"I am a businessman, Detective Hollins, and all this attention is bad for my business. If my international contacts think that I am working in the Wild West, they have less confidence that I can handle my end of any agreements." Arkady was carefully laying out his position.

"Profits are down?" Hollins was dismissive.

"Yes, and you have a shooting war like you haven't seen in your career. The police have been powerless to stop the killings. Your impotence must be embarrassing for your department."

Hollins replied, "I've got to admit it, Valnikov, you have balls asking for this sit-down."

"Detective Hollins, isn't it in both our best interests that this war ends and things return to normal as soon as possible? I am not asking for anything personal from you. I expect you to do your job."

"Damn right. I will come after you again and again and again until I get you."

"Thank you for saying that, Hollins. That is exactly why I chose to meet with you. It is important that I know that I am talking to an honest cop. I also remember when you arrested me. You had a solid case against me; however, my friends talked to somebody who talked to somebody, and you know what happened."

"All too well. It feels like yesterday that I found out that my best evidence against you was stolen from the evidence room during the trial."

"I don't know who the inside man is, but I think you will find out who it is if you keep looking into the murders at the gentlemen's club and of the reporter. They are connected, I believe."

The muffins arrived, both split in half, grilled with an unhealthy amount of butter slathered on top. Both men sat silently chewing and thinking. Fresh coffee was poured, and they were left alone again.

"I know what you are thinking, Detective. Why am I changing my tune now? Why didn't I tell you this when you first questioned me? Things changed between now and then. My group employed an accountant to keep track of our business for the Old Man. Shortly after the Old Man died, the murders at the club occurred, and then the reporter died. I believe the accountant went missing around the time shortly after the reporter's death. It's all connected somehow."

"A warrant has been issued for the arrest of the man believed to be responsible for the reporter's death."

"You are not convinced though, are you, Detective Hollins?" Arkady asked while prodding him for a reaction. Hollins made the slightest perceptible shrug while swallowing his food before washing it down with more coffee. "I heard on the news that the reporter's friend is being sought for it. I think I may have more information for you that ties the killings together, but you can never say you learned this from me."

"And why not?" Hollins asked.

"You have a leak in your organization, and it will get me killed if you do." Arkady tersely replied.

"What makes you think that?"

"A man visited Mr. Sullivan's tent just hours before his arrest warrant was to be executed. He was seen running from the explosions. I believe the man went there to kill Mr. Sullivan before Sullivan could be arrested and possibly tell the police what he knew." Arkady could see Hollins poker face. "Whoever killed the reporter didn't get what he wanted and went after Mr. Sullivan thinking that he now had the information. The killer was tipped off about the impending arrest."

Hollins wiped his mouth with his napkin and signaled the elderly woman who was their server for the check. "That's a stretch."

"Really? You think that it was a coincidence that Sullivan was not there, but yet he set up a fireworks display to go off during the middle of a blizzard?"

"And how would you know that?"

"Do you think that we do not do our own homework when it comes to things impacting our livelihood and maybe our lives? Have you forgotten, Detective Hollins, that it is open season for organized criminals?" Arkady wasn't about to play his hole card. Not here and not now.

Hollins got up to leave, and Arkady stood up as well.

"It's a slippery slope doing business with the Devil, Mr. Valnikov. We will keep investigating organized crime without the help of organized criminals."

"What, you don't use paid informants, you don't flip smaller fish and put them in the witness protection to get the bigger fish? I watch reruns of *Goodfellas*, you know."

Neither man had moved for the check or the door.

"What are you proposing, Mr. Valnikov?"

"I am an anonymous informant. You never met me. You don't know me. I give you information, and if it checks out, it may help you stop all the killings and business goes back to usual so you can still try to put me in jail." Arkady smiled.

Hollins smiled back and picked up the check. "You can go fuck yourself."

CHAPTER TWENTY-NINE

Willie's job with the Delaware River Waterfront Corporation was to clean out the debris that floated downstream and ended up snagged on anything along Penn's Landing. The Delaware runs over 400 miles from the New York Catskills and dumps into the Atlantic Ocean. Sometimes along the way, all sorts of debris, especially after storms, comes to rest at this tourist attraction. Willie was having trouble lifting, with his long extension hook, the plastic-wrapped object that snagged onto the USS *Becuna*, a WWII submarine on permanent display there. He strained to lift and disengage this trash from the sub. He called for help, and the rest of his group assembled to assist with the removal.

Several workers now attached two more hooks and began pulling as well. The plastic was slowly ripped away from the object and the sub. However, Willie's hook was embedded in what looked like a rolled-up carpet. All the workers now strained to push and pull Willie's hook, and with their best heave, the carpet unrolled ten feet above the water, and a human body fell out and floated up against the hull of the sub.

Their screams could be heard for a couple hundred feet that bitterly cold February morning.

Police divers and homicide detectives were called. A floater was a news story, and the media arrived while the scene was being processed. Wes Thompson was the lead detective, and once the body was lifted out of the water, the rug and remaining plastic were collected, and the scene photography was completed, he met the medical examiner under the tent set up at the scene. The elderly white male was clothed, and plastic had covered up both ends of the rug keeping hungry fish from nibbling on his scalp or extremities. The freezing water had not decomposed the body in its tightly wrapped cocoon. No identification was found on the man. The body was removed to the medical examiner's office on University Avenue.

Protocols were followed for taking off the clothing and photographing the injuries. The man had been beaten to death. Both patellas were crushed, and tibias snapped. His tongue was severed and stuffed down his throat. This was just the external examination. Thompson focused on the tattoos. He was not an expert in tattoos, but recognized a familiar pattern and left with his cell phone to his ear.

The medical examiner was new to the office and new to performing autopsies alone. Davina completed her examination and was finishing her dictation, while a tech hosed off the slab and cleaned up around the station. She had only been with the office for a couple of months and assisted in the autopsy of a man with similar tattoos and remembered that case.

She stopped dictation in mid-sentence and went back over the logs and quickly found the case. She brought up the files on her screen and put the photos of the tattoos side by side. She made screenshots of the close-ups and the facial of the unidentified man and sent an email to all the cops listed for both cases. This unidentified corpse had similar ink as the man found shot in the face at the Harbison Ave. Sports Bar and Grille. She stood up, stretched and looked at the next three sheeted gurneys parked at her station.

"Hey, Mike, you gotta minute?" The detective got through on the first ring.

"Yeah, what's up?" Hollins answered even though it was early evening.

"Did you see the email?"

"No, some of us have real jobs, you know."

"You know that fish bait they pulled out of the river this morning?" the detective asked.

"Yeah, I heard about it."

"He had the same tattoos as our Russian guy who was getting his knob gobbled when he got himself killed at the strip club last month. I think there's a connection."

"Not every Russkie is a gangster. You can't shove every untimely death onto my plate."

"Mike, the guy was rolled up in a rug. He didn't jump off the Betsy Ross."

"Oh?"

"Worse. The rug was wrapped in plastic and preserved the body pretty good. He was systematically beaten to death, and his tongue was cut off and jammed down his throat."

"Ok, I get it, I get it. You just destroyed my appetite. I guess this won't be the last take-out dinner that I throw away while working. Can you send me a facial? I'll see what I can do."

Something just came to the surface that you need to know about. Vlad's new burner smartphone read.

"Okay, Valnikov, you have my attention. Talk to me."

"Detective Hollins, don't forget my business is the waterfront. Nothing happens there, without me knowing about it." Arkady was well aware of the man in the rug, and his assumption about the accountant's fate was almost inevitable.

"Let's just say that I needed a little more assurance that you weren't trying to blow smoke up my ass."

"I assure you, Detective. I have no time for games. I don't reach out to anyone in the government to pull their chain."

They were sitting in their separate vehicles on the Lower Merion side of City Line Avenue in a WaWa parking lot.

"Can you promise me anonymity, Detective?"

"Yes, I can, Arkady." Using his first name for the first time Arkady noted. "If it weren't for good upstanding citizens that supplied information anonymously, law enforcement efforts would be significantly impeded." With that said, Hollins handed Arkady his cell phone with the morgue photo of the accountant.

Arkady nodded.

Without much fanfare, Arkady handed Hollins back his phone along with a slip of paper. "His name and address are there. At his apartment, you will find an interesting newspaper article on the end table next to his reading chair. The second address is the Old Man's house, wherein the basement you should find fibers to match the carpet, and you will discover the accountant's glasses. The third place is where the Old Man would dump things into the river. You may get lucky there as well."

"If I didn't know any better, I'd say you had something to do with this."

"No, I just did what any good detective would do. When he went missing, I went to his apartment and went to the last place of business and then I went to the most likely place that I knew where a rug and its contents could go for a swim."

Hollins took it all in. "I'll check it out, but I think you are still holding back."

"Detective, find the man that did this. When you do, you will find the man behind most of the slaughter, including the death of the reporter. I am sticking my neck out here. If we could handle this ourselves, we would, but you have more resources to do the job."

Arkady rolled away from the gas station convenience store and took a circuitous route to his home. He was sure that he had no tail. He lived behind a gated driveway on the Philadelphia Main Line. It was late when he walked through his mansion to the solarium that enclosed the swimming pool and pool house.

Sully could watch Arkady's approach on the security camera monitors from the turn onto the driveway, through the garage and house and along the marble tiled pool deck.

"How'd it go?" Sully asked.

"It is confirmed that the man pulled out of the Delaware was the accountant."

"Your friend?"

"No, not really. More like a grumpy co-worker always demanding more timely reports and better documentation of expenses. He was the Old Man's trusted confidant and did every-thing the Old Man asked."

"And the detective?"

"He said he would try to connect the dots between the gentle-men's club murder, the accountant, and your friend Mr. Menke."

"You took quite a risk, Arkady."

Arkady shrugged. "It's hard to believe that I actually am a police informant."

"Do you trust him?"

"Enough to tell him what I suspect happened to the accoun-tant. He would like to see me go to jail for a long time. He made no attempts to hide his dislike or to elicit a bribe. When we spoke last, I made it clear to him that there is a leak in his department and that my identity cannot be known."

Sully replied, "I wasn't sure of your motives until now, Arkady."

Arkady understood Sully's reluctance. He was a gangster after all.

"I just discovered this while you were away. I think this is why the accountant and Stew died." Sully took the thumb drive that Stew had hidden in his prized 35mm camera and dropped into his birthday bag that night. He inserted the thumb drive into the laptop, and the scene from the club played though with the sound turned up at full volume.

When it was over, Sully looked at Arkady and said, "That is the man who tried to kill me."

"Vladislav Balderis," Arkady replied.

CHAPTER THIRTY

"It's not like I didn't invite the wrath of my supervisor," Marsha said to her brother. He was seated across from her at a rare lunch date in City Tavern. He said he had some good stuff for her.

"Yeah, I circled back on the intelligence that sent you on that wild goose chase. It was bogus. I'm sorry," he said. "Seems like my sources were trying to slough off that all these takedowns, rub-outs and retaliation hits were homegrown. Each group in town is pointing their fingers at the other guy. So, some wild story about the New York Russians making a turf grab was just rumors without any substance," Nick said.

"Don't you usually vet the intelligence before passing it on?" she asked.

"You aren't going to like this, Marsh, but everybody I'm dialed into at the Fusion center is Domestic Security and Counter-Terrorism first, and Organized Crime is a tie for second with every other crime. I passed it on because it was a thread that came from usually reliable sources. Turns out it was just idle chatter. Sorry."

"It just goes to show you how much OC has taken a backseat

to Homeland Security. Seems like that dead reporter was right on the money," Marsha offered.

"There you go again," Nick said, doing his best Ronald Reagan impression. "Do you think you're a little obsessive there, kiddo?"

Little sister replied, "How hard is it to find a skid row drunk, Nick? The guy blew his tent up, his family hasn't seen him and it's the dead of winter. Do you think he knows something more about all this and is hiding out? Maybe somebody could talk him in, and we might find out what really happened."

"I thought the Bureau told you to focus on the wiseguys and forget the reporter. Isn't there enough work to do with all these bodies dropping?"

True enough, Marsha thought. "My squad is up to their eyeballs. One guy has put his papers in for a retirement on his birthday next month. Another is threatening to hang up the spurs if OC doesn't return to being a cozy pre-retirement gig soon. My boss is feeling the heat, and he's adding the pressure."

They sat in silence while the French onion soup was taken away and the lobster rolls were set down in front of them. Both picked at the meat and left the lobster-soaked grilled buns for last. Small talk about family, the Phillies and who the Eagles were going to pick first in the draft passed the time. Both used the bathrooms, then Nick picked up the check. They had to go back to work.

Outside, they both got ready to face the icy sleet pelting the awning above them like machine gun fire. "Listen," Nick said, "We fished a guy out of the Delaware, and he was the Old Russian Guy's right-hand man. I'm told that he was trying to make a power play and took out the competition and got cute by making it look like it was the Sicilians. He visited the reporter when he thought the reporter had something on him. When the Russians found out what he was doing, they punched his ticket.

But it is too late, the genie is out of the bottle. They can't say that they're sorry."

"What about Sullivan?" Marsha asked.

"Homicide doesn't want to admit they may have the wrong guy with Sullivan. We will find Sullivan and get him to plea to manslaughter, given his alcoholism and PTSD."

"That's it, huh? Looks to me that everything is wrapped with a nice little bow," Marsha said.

"What's the problem?" Nick asked testily.

"Christ, we barely knew who Vasily Pavlichenko was, and now there is another Russian that wasn't on our family org charts powerful enough to start a shooting war. He had the brains to plan and the hitters to execute what looks a military operation. What's his name?"

"Don't know yet. Doesn't look like his dental was done in America and his prints are clean."

"A freaking John Doe, more like Ivan Doe, lovely." Marsha sighed. "Do you have a picture at least?"

"I'll text it to you," Nick said.

Marsha walked back to her office and settled down at her desk when her phone pinged a text message in. She figured that Nick beat her back to his office. It was Mike Hollins.

I left my sunglasses in your car and need them for my Florida vacation. Can I come by and pick them up?

"Florida my ass, Mike, what's up with the secret visit?" They were sitting in Marsha's rag top Mustang in the expensive, but dry parking garage where she parked it year-round.

"I've got a name for one of the Russians that went to the Old Man's wake."

He gave her a 5 x 8 photo of the accountant in death. "Sergei Maltsarov, he was the Old Man's accountant."

Marsha shuffled her pictures of the Old Man's inner circle that she had taken off the board at Mike's request following the cryptic message. To date, she had not placed a name with the face of him as the man who was the last one to walk into the Old Man's wake, even after the bikers.

"He was in the water for some time before they unraveled him from a rug. He'd been beaten to death and his tongue was stuffed down his throat." Mike explained.

"You came over here to tell me this?" Marsha wondered if there was something more to this and she didn't want to mention what her brother had given her as a form of an apology for bad intel just a few hours earlier.

"This was on the reading stand in his living room. Mike slid another picture over to her, this time of the Stew Menke article on Organized Crime."

"So you think they're connected?"

"Yeah, this is why I am here on the QT. I think the guy that killed them both is the guy that offed the Russian in the Strip Club. I am trying to figure out if he might have been the guy that went to Sullivan's tent just hours before our arrest warrant was to be served."

This was too much to take in and weigh against what her brother told her at the same time. Marsha's head was spinning. She gave him a confused look.

"Hey Marsha, I am just finding out that Sullivan had a visitor, who was seen running away from his tent when it went up like the Fourth of July. Remember, Homicide says that Menke's killer is Sullivan. Nobody bothered to copy me on the field reports about what happened at F troop until I started connecting the dots on the accountant.

"Why did your unit get called in?"

"A detective was copied in by the M.E. on the photos of tattoos on both the Russian Capo and the accountant. Seems that they spent time in the same Russian prison gangs." Mike brought out the comparison photos and handed them to her.

"But that doesn't tell me why you needed to look at what happened in F Troop the other night?"

"Marsha, I already told you enough. I don't want to get into a pissing contest with Homicide. They want Sullivan for Menke's murder. I can't run with that piece. I am gonna focus on who killed the capo, the girl, and the accountant. You want to solve Menke's murder. I'm handing you a hot potato. You can hold it or drop it."

Hollins left her there to sort through it all. Did the accountant order the capo's death and get to go for a swim for his ordering the end of a newspaper reporter, or was he dropped in the river by somebody that tortured Menke and is now targeting Sullivan?

Her migraine was starting earlier than usual.

CHAPTER THIRTY-ONE

The sun rose with the promise of a mild day. The memorial service was packed. Stew's daughter, her husband, and his ex-wife sat in the first row directly in front of the podium. Sully recognized them by the framed pictures that Stew had in his living room at the apartment.

He and Arkady argued about coming to the service. The Philadelphia police still had an active warrant out for his arrest in Stew's murder. They finally came up with a compromise. Dressed as a Hasidic Jew with a wig and false beard of dark hair, Sully was accompanied by Arkady's office manager at the freight office, similarly dressed. They made a homely pair. They arrived at the lecture hall on the Temple University campus minutes before the start.

A photo montage was streaming on the screen behind the podium with soft music playing. Stew's signature photo sat on an easel stage left. The hat, the battered typewriter and the cigarette dangling from his lips with Stew staring at the field from the press box at Veterans Stadium had been replayed on the news. His employer, *The Daily Sun*, had run it a few times since Stew's death. From the back row, Sully surveyed the scene. There was an absence of flowers as the family had asked that all donations be made to the Ellis Long Hunger/Homeless Project. Sully recognized many former Phillies in the crowd. Doc Barnes, the Phillies manager, was there along with Ellis and Joe DiNatale. They were probably Stew's closest friends. Spring training was less than two weeks away.

When Sully worked the soup kitchen with Stew, he would see them there occasionally. The woman sitting next to DiNatale looked familiar but from where?

He knew he needed to be there to pay his respects. He was resolved to confront his feelings and not drown them in alcohol. He was taking his meds, eating well, reading the AA big book and sleeping like a baby in Arkady's pool house while they planned their next steps to trap Stew's killer. It was this single-minded pursuit that made it possible for him to resist the urge to get shit-faced and fall into the abyss again. His attention was drawn to Stew's daughter's approach to the podium as the service began.

Vlad and his crew had been set up around the memorial service on nearby city streets with a few of his younger men posed as curious journalism students inside the hall. All were connected with comms. Vlad sat in his bullet-proof black Chevy Suburban nearby, knowing that this was necessary. He planned to take Sullivan out before the Fugitive Squad could apprehend him. His burns had not healed fully, but the incessant throbbing pain had subdued to a constant ache.

He was aggravated that he could not take out his frustration at the martial arts studio and noticed that his anger mounted without the release of intense jiu-jitsu workouts. His plans to cut a new deal with the other OC families in town was on hold while he tended to this distraction. This wasn't part of the plan. From the time that the Old Man died until now he had complete control over all the outcomes, save for the surprise by the Zoo and this man Sullivan.

Hard-boiled Homicide Detective Wes Montgomery stood along the side of the auditorium closest to the street. That they had not apprehended Sullivan to date was not his fault. He was there at the service to let the dead man's family and the public know that the police hadn't forgotten. He had argued with his superiors about arresting Sullivan while they had him under guard at the hospital. Yes, Sullivan had told others that he was the last person to see Menke alive, but it wasn't until the bat came back with his prints on it, did they decide to upgrade him from a person of interest to a suspect. That pain in the ass Hollins from OC had argued that Sullivan provided them with an alternative suspect, and sure enough, the delay over testing on the red tracksuit fibers found on the bat and in the victim's wound allowed Sullivan to escape.

What Sullivan looked like now was not a mystery to them, as the Hospital Director of Security Murphy and the floor nurses described him as having shaved his head and face. The police composite artist made a sketch, and that got printed and aired in the media. What if he had that information sooner? He scanned the audience as the eulogies droned on. He recognized some of the faces of the Phillies, and then he centered his attention on the blonde next to Phillie's favorite son, Joe DiNatale.

She texted Jingles the night before that she was going to a funeral. She didn't think she needed to bring back a church bulletin to prove it. She spotted DiNatale as she was walking in. He was surrounded by Phillie's contingent milling at the entrance, before taking their seats. Marsha had shared a magical night in college with him after they escaped a fraternity party unscathed. She was a sorority sister, and he was a freshman pledge to the frat. Nearly twenty years later, she had badged her way into a charity event and learned that he had not forgotten their night many years ago either. DiNatale became an overnight sensation, and curiously, a friend with the acerbic sports writer Menke. Had anybody asked him if Stew had talked about his organized crime investigations? The focus on Sullivan was almost tunnel vision. Menke had no family local as his ex and daughter flew in from the West Coast, but who were his friends? She was there to get those answers, and now she was sitting next to one of them.

When the service was over, she rushed to the people that had spoken and asked if they would talk with her later about Stew's still-unsolved murder. A card from an FBI agent established why and helped them to nod their heads. She wasn't going to conduct interviews in this setting. At her request, DiNatale lingered until she finished.

"I think that Stew was on to something with what was about to happen with the explosion of organized crime violence in the past five weeks. How was he with you, Joe?"

He paused before answering to let a Hasidic couple walk past them. "He was troubled. I asked and he said that he may have bitten off more than he could chew with the articles about the wiseguys."

"How so?" she asked.

"Besides the nut jobs, he was getting some excellent tips and seemed to be consumed by them."

"How was he?"

"Paranoid and nervous. Something was eating him, but he said that he was going to blow the roof off with his story. Last time I saw him he said that I would have to read about it in the papers. I was shocked when I heard that he was killed, but not really surprised."

"That's how the math added up for you; that they got to him first?"

DiNatale nodded.

Marsha said, "The cops like Joe Sullivan for Stew's murder. Did you ever meet him?"

He nodded again. "Seemed like a harmless enough drunk. I've been around them all my life. I don't think he could have done it."

"Cop's ever talk to you?"

"Yeah, they showed me the picture of my special home run bat that I gave to Stew. Made me sick to my stomach that it was used to kill him."

They stood in silence on the sidewalk for a right amount of time. An ambulance siren could be heard approaching and receding in the distance. A flock of pigeons pecking at the grass in the quadrangle between buildings took off and circled overhead.

"It's kinda personal for me too." She played the voice message that Stew left for her.

Marsha's eyes teared up as she stood to face DiNatale.

"Shit," he said.

"Double shit," she replied, and she closed the distance to wipe her tears on his shoulder and then she felt his warm and tender embrace.

As they let go of each other. She returned to being Marsha the gunslinger, put on her sunglasses over reddened eyes and said, "Believe it or not I have another memorial service to go to on this same case. Make no mistake about it, I will get the guy that who killed Stew. I owe it to him."

"No doubt, Marsha, no doubt."

"See ya, D. Gotta go."

Sully pulled the female FBI agent's card from his pocket as Arkady's office manager drove the speed limit in the rented black Crown Vic with heavy tints on the Roosevelt Boulevard towards the northeast section of Philly.

Genrikh Yukushev, Leonid and the other capo's huddled with Arkady at the same funeral home where the Old Man's wake was held. Now they stared at the casket of the accountant. Arkady had embraced each man, his phone did not beep. Sully, who was still in disguise, was sitting outside in the Crown Vic with the wireless receiver equipment showing no activity from the bug scanner Arkady was wearing. Arkady needed to see if any of them would openly admit their suspicion of Bad Vlad before they had a surprise visit, or worse, if any of them was a wearing a wire.

"Belize, my ass. We know who did this," Arkady said. "Which of us is next?"

These rich and powerful men were quarrelsome, and the conversation was contentious. Nobody would come right and say that Vlad should be eliminated, but they all agreed that the bloodshed had to stop so that that business could return to normal.

Marsha had told Hollins where to park to watch the front entrance of the funeral home. He just finished copying down the plate on the black Crown Vic being driven by a woman with a man in the passenger seat fiddling with a laptop in the parking lot. By the way they were dressed, they appeared Jewish. He didn't know what religion the floater was. Maybe Eastern Orthodox Christian, given some of the framed pictures he found in the accountant's apartment. He had already noted all of the other arrivals, and by design was going to confront them all after the service. Only Valnikov knew about it, and they talked about how he would act particularly pissed off at Valnikov. That wouldn't be all that diffi-cult. He watched as Marsha's plain vanilla cargo van circled the building and took up the surveillance position on the other side of the building by the parking lot. *Do I tell her about Valnikov?* he thought.

CHAPTER THIRTY-TWO

From the outside, it looked like a hothouse. The glass walls and sloped roof were fogged over, and patio lighting gave it an otherworldly feel. Inside the half-sized Olympic swimming pool was surrounded by empty patio chairs, tables and chaises lounges that silently waited for Arkady's summer parties. The pool house, which stored the glass panels during the warmer months, also had a shower and changing room. There Sully and Arkady sat on an Ikea futon that doubled as Sully's bed next to a mini-fridge, microwave and hot-plate.

Arkady watched as Sully slowly removed the wig and beard that had been taped to the stubble growing on his face and scalp. Sully winced as the tape did not easily let go. The long black coat and hat, slacks, black tie and white shirt hung neatly nearby. Sully sat in cargo pants and an olive drab T-shirt. The warm humidity made for a comfortable closeness. Arkady had changed from his mourning clothes to designer slacks and an open-collared dress shirt.

"If I did not know that Hollins was acting, I would have said he was a real prick," Arkady offered. "He came at me hard and gave the others the chance to supply him with Vlad's name, but none of my comrades wanted to be a 'cooperator.' It's not in their DNA, and it made me wonder why I went to him in the first place."

"Having second thoughts, Arkady?" Sully asked.

"Knowing the police have a leak and realizing what Vlad is capable of concerns me. Dying prematurely is a hazard in my line of work, so I am mostly risk-averse to hastening my own demise. I had no problem with tying the death of the accountant to the death of your friend as it is beneficial to both of us. We now know what tied them together. I stopped short of explaining that to Hollins because the feed from the club to the Old Man's computer was secret. It wouldn't take the detective long to figure out that I was holding out on him."

"Maybe we don't have to hold onto this secret much longer," Sully said. He tossed a business card onto the wooden freight crate serving as a coffee table.

Arkady looked at the card and stood up. "You talked to the FBI at the memorial service?"

Sully could see the alarm on his face. "No. No. Arkady, relax. She and Hollins came to visit me in the hospital with another cop when I was mostly out of it. I found her card in my hospital gown and remembered her when I saw her there. It was weird though. I'm still trying to figure it out."

"Explain." Arkady still was standing. His alarm was palpable.

"I'm at the memorial service, and I see a bunch of former and present Phillies come in, and she was with one of them. Stew was a sportswriter before he went back to his first love, and that was the crime beat. We used to talk about both a lot. That's how he got all the memorabilia. I couldn't figure out where I knew her from. At first, I just thought she was a girlfriend or wife, but that didn't feel right. She was a mourner like the rest of us. She was just like me or anybody else there. Later, I saw her murmuring outside of the service to the famous pitcher that had given Stew the bat which they found with my finger-prints on it."

"The murder weapon." Arkady nodded his head.

"As we walked by her on the sidewalk, I could see her talking to him, and when I heard her voice and what she was asking, it all clicked with me." Sully paused. "But something else was there. I still can't figure it out. They were comfortable sitting side by side in the hall, and he waited for her while she offered her condolences to the family. How did this FBI agent and ballplayer know each other? I'm still trying to figure that out."

"Maybe they both knew your friend." Arkady softened and sat back down.

"He was a sportswriter and a crime writer. He wrote about baseball, and he would have to talk to cops and the people investigating the mob." Sully mulled that over. "No, she moved in for a hug."

"It was a memorial service, Sully, people do that sort of thing," Arkady said.

"She was there for a reason, and it was personal."

"And you want to talk to her?" Arkady asked.

"Do you think the Feds have a leak too?" Sully volleyed back.

"Not that I am aware of. They move around the country, seem to be better educated and better paid than local police departments. We have our best luck with the policeman with personal problems or who work vice and street-level drug crime. They are more pliable. It doesn't happen overnight."

Sully thought about that for a minute. Arkady was a business-man, and his business depended on good guys looking the other way or tipping them off when something was about to go down.

"What if I walked the thumb drive and the phone he dropped to her? I'd be safe in federal custody while they connected Balderis to the accountant and Stew with the deaths at the strip club. Don't forget, I saw him walk into Stew's apartment building."

"He matches the general description of the guy that ran away from your tent that night," Arkady added.

Sully said, "That's right, and maybe it ties him to the other killings that they arrested the South Philly guy on."

Arkady and Sully sat quietly listening to the whirring of the pool filter as the idea floated like the plastic yellow duck toys drifting on the pool's surface.

Arkady said, "Once you give yourself up, you lose control of the outcome. We have time before we decide. My plan has fewer moving parts."

CHAPTER THIRTY-THREE

They talked more about the plans as Arkady drove up the Jersey Turnpike to New York. Sully was dressed like a successful businessman with his Jeff cap, lined raincoat, sports coat, buttoned down pressed shirt, slacks and Italian dress shoes. In his pocket was the stolen identity of a prosperous Center City merchant who used his credit card at a Russian-held gas station. The driver's license was a little more difficult, but Yukushev's backroom boys used a machine that re-produced the embedded holograph images perfectly, having stolen it from the DMV loading docks in Harrisburg.

Arkady once again completed a bug sweep on his clothes and SUV before crossing the Delaware near Trenton. Not knowing when his "bodyguard" would show up in his driveway or at his freight transfer offices by the river was problematic. He came to realize when his minder was not with him, some sort of mischief involving guns and gangs would be reported on by the news media.

The farmlands of Central Jersey gave way to oil and gas tanks in Linden, then monstrous cranes loading and off-loading shipping containers in Elizabeth and then followed by the constant drone of aircraft landing and taking off from Newark airport.

Shortly, they saw the Empire State Building and the Statue of Liberty as they made their way to the Hudson and the Holland Tunnel. Coming out of the darkness and into the morning smog-free light of lower Manhattan, they were immediately intimidated by the rush hour hustle. Center City Philly was a walk in the park compared to the press of cars, trucks and cabbies going about their lawful acts of commerce.

The shop was tucked away below street level between a clothing boutique and vegan restaurant in walking distance of Union Square and the Ironbound Building. There was no signage announcing that this was an electronics shop or a store of any sort. The intercom answered with a male voice to Arkady's buzz. "What do you want?"

Arkady replied with the code phrase. "Only to find happiness in the smallest of things." He then smiled to both cameras.

A click later, he and Sully were in the vestibule, and only after the door closed behind them did the interior door click open. Again, two more cameras observed their movements.

They pushed their way into the brightly lit subterranean room. A thick-waisted older man with a jeweler's magnifying glass and a bright halo light sat hunched over the long display case. One hand held the circuit board and the other a soldering gun. It was a tricky maneuver and both men remained silent until he finished the operation.

"Marrying German optics with Japanese wireless technology," he said with an Eastern European accent. When they cooled, he placed the pieces smaller than the palm of his meaty hand into the slotted interior of a dull black box with the direct contacts to the lithium nine-volt battery in its base.

It was no longer than a deck of cards or wider than a pack of cigarettes. Setting it on the display top, he turned on the computer monitor for them all to see and with a joystick was able to move the camera lenses to magnify in and out but also to move it left to right about 135 degrees. High Definition and Color. Another set up was on the table. "That one is low light that is almost as good as infrared. It is for night-time operations. That's next."

Arkady said, "Still having fun with the toys."

"Keeps me out of trouble, Arkady. Let me show you what I have for you." He reached down below the case and brought out the goodies. "Here are the comms you requested. We had to sacrifice some distance for stealth." He placed the flesh colored earbud in Arkady's right ear and the ivory colored voice-activated microphone on his top shirt button. He gave the standard Israeli executive protection headset to Sully and told him to walk into the back room. The portly Pole walked down and back the length of the display case and gave a ten count in a normal speaking voice. Then he asked Arkady to do the same. Finally, he called Sully to provide a ten count. Arkady nodded and talked back to Sully.

Sully came out from the back room and said, "You both were loud and clear, but how would it work if there was background noise?"

The three men walked out onto the street. Sully trailed the others by a good 15-20 yards as they made their way to Union Square and the hustle-bustle of lower Manhattan. Buses letting off passengers, delivery trucks backing up with the annoying beep-beep-beep and buskers twanging on guitars and singing in the frosty air all came into Sully's earpiece, but when Arkady spoke, he was able to make him out clearly, Grzegorz not so much. With a line of sight, they could communicate without static for the length of a football field.

Shaking off the cold, the men returned to the showroom. "Here are the two covert security cameras you asked for along with a miniature receiver and hard drive." The cameras were miniaturized and had Velcro mounting sleeves. They transmitted a wide-angle picture with sound to the receiver that had all the look and feel of a standard cell phone with a simple mounting attachment. "Both are motion activated, and the battery life is a good 48 hours. Here are the spare batteries." Sully and Arkady were handed coin-shaped discs. He showed them how to open up the back with the edge of the battery. When he powered everything up, the screen came alive, and a red light came on showing the images were being recorded on split screens. "Flip to channel 2 on your comm, sir."

Sully was able to hear Grzegorz do a ten count as he moved the cameras to the opposite ends of the room. "That is downright scary," he said.

"Go to channel 3. Arkady, walk and give him a ten count."

Sully was able to hear Arkady clearly, and both of the camera microphones picked up as Arkady moved back and forth. "I suggest you keep it on this setting."

He reached into a different bag and produced the bullet-proof torso and side panels under-armor. "I had to get a seamstress to work on it just for you, Arkady. They didn't have a Russian Bear size in stock."

Looking at everything on top of the display case, it was a significant amount of specialized equipment custom-made by this crafty craftsman. Arkady looked up and asked, "What do I owe you for all this?" without reaching for his wallet.

Grzegorz waved him away and acted insulted. "For all the favors I have asked of you over the years, Arkady, you never asked me for a dollar. I will be still in your debt until I breathe my last breath."

Sully and Arkady picked up the nondescript nameless shopping bags, thanked the man and found their way to the valet park nearby.

When they got in the SUV and started towards the Holland, Sully said, "This is Plan B, Arkady, right?"

"Said the pig to the Chicken," Arkady replied.

"What?"

"It is like a bacon and egg breakfast; the pig is committed, the chicken is involved. You want to stay alive and not spend the rest of that life in jail. I just want things to get back to normal. We have looked at both ideas and know the pros and cons. In the end, we must go the way you feel most comfortable. If it doesn't work, my chicken will most likely keep laying eggs, but you, my friend, will not have a second chance once you give yourself up."

Neither man was interested in passing the time with idle banter. Both had much on their minds. Sully directed Arkady to the quiet suburban neighborhood of post-WWII cookie-cutter housing. The original Cape Cod designs on quarter-acre lots in Bensalem had as many alterations and changes as the town permitted over the past seventy years. He parked around the corner after driving past Sully's home.

No one was home. Tracey was at work, and Brittany was in aftercare. It was getting close to dusk when he walked through his rear neighbor's yard and tried his back door. He found that his key still worked. Into the basement and then the crawlspace, he found his footlocker. Everything was in order. A few minutes later, on Sully's signal, Arkady pulled up in front of the rear neighbor's house, and Sully got in the passenger door before anyone noticed. The gun case held his scoped deer-hunting rifle, ammo, 1911 Colt Automatic pistol, and the gun cleaning solvents and oils. The Plan B equipment list was complete.

CHAPTER THIRTY-FOUR

"Line 2, Marsha," someone yelled over the divider to her. She was busy studying the ballistic reports on the latest retaliation killing of Dominicans by Columbians in Mayfair and distractedly reached for the phone.

"This is Special Agent O'Shea, who am I speaking with?" she said automatically while still scanning the reports.

"This is Joseph Sullivan. You came to visit me in the hospital when I was kind of in and out of it. You and two cops were trying to question me about Stew Menke's death."

Marsha sat up and reached for a legal pad almost knocking over her Hardrock Miami insulated water carafe. "How do I know who this really is?"

"You slipped your card into my hospital gown where I found it and kept it. I remembered what you looked like when I saw you outside of Stew's memorial service talking to Joe DiNatale. He was Stew's friend, and I met him a couple of times at the soup kitchen."

"You were there?" She tried remembering all the faces that day.

"I went to pay my respects, Agent O'Shea."

She remembered the straggly beard and unkempt hair. She had seen the composite sketch of him completely shorn and remarked to Ramit how different they looked. She was drawing a blank. "There were a lot of sad people there that day," Marsha admitted.

"Angry people too. And cops looking to see if I would show up."

"You fooled everybody. You calling me to brag about it?" she asked.

"No. No, not at all. I have a bunch of reasons why I wanted to speak with you. First, I think you know I didn't kill Stew. The cops want to arrest me for it, and I can't go to them."

She sidestepped Sullivan's correct assumption. "Why not give yourself up? The longer you stay in hiding, the worse it looks for you." Marsha said.

"Not to the cops. I would not make bail, and I'd get knifed in lock-up before I could make it to trial."

"Why would somebody kill you in prison?"

"That's the second reason I wanted to talk to you. I believe the man they found floating in the river gave something to Stew and that is what got them both killed."

Marsha wondered how he could say that. "What man in the river are you talking about? People drown in the Schuylkill all the time."

"Don't play dumb with me, Agent O'Shea. I can hang up, and you will never hear from me again. You went to two memorial services that day, and you know damn well which man I am talking about."

Marsha was flabbergasted. How does this guy know so much? She regained her composure quickly and said, "You are wanted for murder. The cops think you killed Stew in a drunken blackout. You are telling me it had to do with organized crime. How did you make the connection? How did you know I was at the other service later that day?"

"Lie to me again, and I hang up."

Marsha said, "I can't give you information from our investigations. I have no basis to trust you or trade information with you. If I can tell you something, it will be truthful, or I will say I can't disclose it. That's the best I can do. Now, how do you know that floater was connected to Stew?"

There was silence on the other end. A long agonizing silence. Shit, I can't be the one to break the silence. She heard the rustling of the phone, as Sullivan wrestled with his decision.

"Because Stew gave me the evidence in my birthday present bag that night and I didn't know it until after I retrieved it when I got discharged from the hospital."

"Shit!" Marsha exclaimed.

"Yeah, that also explains why somebody tried killing me after I got out and why I won't last long in lock-up," Sullivan said. "After I got cleaned up, it didn't take me long to figure out why somebody would want to kill Stew. It had to do with what he was about to expose. I didn't realize until later that he died protecting a secret. He died protecting me without me even knowing about it. So maybe I had a damn good reason for going to his service, besides the fact that he saw something in me and was one of the few people that treated me like a human being."

"You're right, Mr. Sullivan. I don't think you killed your friend."

Another long pause before he said, "Call me Sully."

"The police department has stopped looking for other suspects. They are zeroed in on you, Sully, but I wasn't so sure."

"It was the man with the red Temple tracksuit. He's the guy that I'm almost positive tried to silence me permanently."

"You set a trap for him, didn't you Sully?" Marsha asked.

"Once I found out I had what was given to Stew, I had to be sure. It didn't take long to get my answer."

"No, it didn't." she said.

Sully said, "Do you think it was a coincidence that he tried to off me before the cops showed up to serve a warrant on my sorry ass?"

She replied, "Not now that you are filling in the puzzle."

"Do you understand why I can't go to the cops now? Somebody tipped off the killer."

Marsha filled in the picture for him. "You would be just another skid-row drunk that gets himself killed on the streets. Your death seals the deal and closes Stew's death without there being a messy trial and defense investigation. You'd go to your grave with the secret that was worth killing three people for."

"Exactly," he replied. "There's more."

"What?"

"I'll tell you when I see you. I will give you his name and at least two more bodies that he is good for." Sully said.

"In exchange for what?"

"Put me in protective custody, have the Feds take over the investigation with what I give you. Promise my safety while you sort this out."

Marsha was never a bureaucrat. Now she had both an opportunity and a problem. They didn't cover this in Quantico, she thought.

How long did she weigh the pros and cons, she did not know as she lost track of time. Finally, her thoughts were interrupted. "Agent O'Shea, are you still there?"

"I don't know how the hell I can do that without stepping on toes and getting a buy-in from my bosses," she answered.

"Does that mean you can't do it?"

"No, Sully, it means that from this point forward, you have to trust me and you can only trust me if I am completely honest with you. I have to think about how to do this while stepping on toes and also pissing off my employer."

"Trade places with me, Agent O'Shea. I'm less than a month

sober, medicating for PTSD and I'm wanted by the cops for a murder that I didn't commit. The man who tortured and killed at least four people is gunning for me too."

"We can't work out the details now, but you need to give me a little time to figure out how I can bring you in."

"I want to hear the whole plan before I agree to come in."

"That's a fair request, Sully," Marsha replied.

"One more thing, Agent O'Shea."

"What's that Sully?"

"It's none of my business what you have going with DiNatale, but I do know that you were mourning for Stew too. It cinched my decision to come to you and turn myself in."

"You're right, Sully, that is none of your business, and you can call me tomorrow on my cell, 215-555-4321 after 4 p.m. I will have an answer for you."

"Okay, fair enough." He disconnected.

CHAPTER THIRTY-FIVE

"It doesn't feel right," Arkady said. He was driving. Wearing an Eagles cap over a ratty green parka, he could have been any other deliveryman.

"I don't like it either," Sully replied. He was disguised this time as a UPS driver with a hat pulled down low. A hand truck loaded with packages would make it all the more believable. He told Marsha he would find her and she would know it was him. If he didn't like the setup, he'd bounce.

Marsha was to meet Sully by the security funnel and metal detectors at the Federal Courthouse downtown. She had a meeting in the morning with an assistant United States attorney on wiretap plans and was instead going to surprise him with a witness seeking custodial protection, claiming that Sully had her under surveillance, intercepted her and then pitched her on the way in.

Sully and Marsha argued about this plan heatedly. She told him she needed to know what cards he was holding. It was evidence that would buy him his protection. Why he shouldn't be turned over to the Philadelphia police on an active murder warrant was even more trickier.

It boiled down to how good was the evidence that Sully held.

That would grease the Federal bureaucracy wheels to hold onto him while rebuffing the police demands for his head on a pike. He finally relented and sent her a five-second SnapChat video of the gun entering the scene of the soon-to-be-dead Russian who was being pleasured at the gentlemen's club. It was enough of a teaser to convince her he had the rest of the goods.

Sully and Arkady had an eyeball on the courthouse entrance. They saw Marsha turn south on Market Street. It was a cloudy and dull gray day. Traffic moved listlessly on the main thorough-fare in shouting distance of the Liberty Bell. It was too early for the tourists and a few minutes before the courthouse would begin accepting the public. Sully wore the earbud and button microphone.

"Ain't nothing to it, but to do it." Sully said, realizing that this may be the last time he saw Arkady. Had they bonded? He and the gangster had a mutual interest. Both had lived up to their bargains. Before exiting the truck, Sully handed Arkady another thumb drive containing the footage two men died for when they tried to protect it. "In case this goes sideways."

Arkady nodded. "Be well, my friend."

They watched Marsha turn into the protected entrance. Since the Oklahoma City Bombing and especially after 9-11, Federal buildings received some questionable artwork in the form of substantial unmovable barriers to prevent another vehicle loaded with explosives from getting too close.

Sully went around back and loaded the boxes that contained discarded computer parts onto the hand truck and began wheeling it towards the courthouse entrance.

"Check, check." Sully tested the mike.

"Check, loud and clear," came Arkady's reply.

Crusty ice and snow piles between parking spaces remained, but the sidewalks were clear. He thumped along moving his head from side to side of the packages that were stacked to eye level.

The walk was slow but steady. He had practiced the day before by doing laps around the pool patio. He had to look the part. He was unarmed and agreed with Marsha that carrying a concealed weapon into a courthouse was not the olive branch the government would be looking for. He began to question that thinking as he scanned for threats. He felt naked without a weapon. This is wrong. What am I walking into?

As he tilted the boxes to drag them in backward through the entrance doors, a Chevy Suburban stopped short of the entrance on the north side of Market, next to the courthouse, while its twin stopped short of the south side of Market across the street.

"Sully, get out of there, it's an ambush." Arkady chirped into his earbud.

Sully stopped and pretended to adjust the boxes. He bent low and started fiddling with the bottom ones. He would rush any attacker if he had to, but the bruiser walked past him to a corner where he began scanning the crowd queuing for the metal detectors. He spotted two more walk in, and they triangulated on Marsha from the corners. Whoever meets with her, dies Sully realized.

"They are wearing comms. Where did they come from?" Sully asked.

"You've got two tinted out Chevrolet Suburbans boxing in the entrance," Arkady replied.

Sully could see Marsha slowly shifting her balance from one foot to the other. She was casually scanning the people coming in. Good thing she doesn't recognize me.

"Do you still have the burner phone?" Sully asked Arkady.

"Yes, why?"

"Fire it up and call in a bomb threat. Wait for me to come out with just the hand truck," Sully said.

Sully pretended to check an old-fashioned paper manifest, counting the boxes and reshuffling them on the ground next to the truck. He watched the security people with interest as they went through purses and backpacks. They would get slaughtered in the cross-fire and were unaware of the trap.

Their radios squawked, and the supervisor leaped to his feet. They huddled quickly to confirm what they just heard. Two ran to the interior of the building and began telling people to leave. The others started shepherding people who had business with the court to slowly walk outside. The word bomb was not mentioned. Then the building's alarms rang and from outside, the sounds of police and fire sirens could be heard.

The bruiser and his companions looked panicked. They were apparently being told to stick with Marsha, who flashed her credentials at the security personnel again. The lobby began to empty out of those who just came in, and now a new flood of employees came clattering down the stairs carrying coats, pocketbooks, and totes. Half empty coffees and iced drinks sloshed in their hands as they bippity-bopped down the stairs. After all, they couldn't throw away their five dollar lattes.

Sully left the packages there and walked briskly with his hand truck into the gaggle of fleeing government employees to the exit, in time to see more of the bruiser's buddies jumping back in the Suburbans.

He quickstepped to the corner as Arkady made a right turn going north and stopped just out of sight of his would-be assassins. Sully leaned the hand truck against a pole then thought twice and slammed it back inside the rear of the empty truck. He calmly got into the passenger seat.

"Our van will be all over the news tonight, we have to ditch it." Sully said.

"The UPS guy's photo will be all of the news too when the bomb squad finds the packages and looks at the video," Arkady replied.

"Gimme the phone." Sully was less than pleasant as his adrenaline turned to anger. He set it down in his lap, as they sat at a traffic light watching emergency vehicles descend on the courthouse.

Arkady moved cautiously on green to make sure they didn't get broad-sided, as he made his way towards a spot along the river where the truck would get toasted. He called his office manager and instructed her to be waiting nearby with a change of clothes for both of them.

Sully typed a text to Marsha. *You are welcome. I just saved a lot of innocent lives. Watch the tapes of the no-necks that walked in after the UPS guy and the two Chevy Suburbans outside. You almost got us killed. Bye.* Sully threw the burner out the window, and it went cartwheeling below the guardrail and into other debris along northbound I-95.

You are welcome. I just saved a lot of innocent lives. Watch the tapes of the no-necks that walked in after the UPS guy and the two Chevy Suburbans outside. You almost got us killed. Bye. Vlad read it on the clone phone in real time just as Marsha was reading it on hers.

CHAPTER THIRTY-SIX

"Explain it to me again."

She looked at her supervisor in the conference room. It had been a long day, and she was bone tired. She read the text from Sully and looked up to acquire the no-necks just as they were beating feet to the exit doors. She kept her hand on her Glock under her blazer.

Using the flock of departing employees as a shield, she watched as they ran to two Chevy Suburbans, which squealed out of sight, just before the arriving emergency responders. She stood there impotently knowing that Sully saved not only her life but many others. How could anyone else have known about this plan? That thought kept running through her head.

"Marsha?" Her supervisor interrupted her train of weary thought.

She looked up at him again. "Sorry, it's been a long day. I had an appointment before court to meet AUSA Wallace Bansley. I am friendly with his secretary Connie and decided to wait for her to ride up with her. She just came back from family leave, and I wanted to ask her about the baby. When the security guys started moving people to the exits, I spotted a couple guys that didn't look right. I followed them out and got the license plate on one of the tinted-out Chevy Suburbans that they got into." She waited. *Keep it tight, don't change your story.*

"And you made yourself a pain in the ass to the point of demanding to watch the videotapes with the squad investigating the bomb threat." Her supervisor Jingles was the first to break the silence. He tried provoking her into making further disclosures. An amateur move, but it was always the first move he made.

"And they made a complaint, and that's why we're here. I get it but that doesn't change the fact that I was onto something."

"It wasn't your case, Agent O'Shea. You were sticking your nose where it didn't belong."

"When minutes count, you are telling me that I had to stand down? Last time I checked we were all playing on the same team."

"You are coming very close to being insubordinate, Agent O'Shea," he warned her.

"I'm sorry. I was just tad bit upset. Somebody just threatened to blow up the building that I was standing in—a federal courthouse, the last time I checked. I wanted to catch the bastards that did it. Can I get back to work now?" They had been over her story several times now, and it wasn't changing.

Jingles looked away and then back to Marsha. "You will be notified of the actions that will be taken on this complaint, Agent O'Shea. This complaint will become a permanent record in your personnel package."

She nonchalantly shrugged and left.

She walked back to her cubicle on the bullpen floor. The office was nearly deserted. Ramit was still there though.

What if I met Sully and tried to badge him through Security? Knowing the setup of the killers from the video, I would have been dead before I reached the elevators along with a whole bunch of other innocent people. I wasn't even expecting an ambush. Fuck!

What if I told Bansley of my plans ahead of time? The less than pleasant chat with Jingles would have been a lot worse. I would have to explain to that asshole why I went around the Philly PD after being told to stand down. I can see the papers in a few months talking about how the former FBI agent went rogue and almost caused a slaughter.

Marsha kept digging deeper into her suffering. She did this often when street work didn't go as planned. Her inner-perfectionist wouldn't allow anything else. Had somebody gotten to the retired AUSA in Florida? No. She was far out of the loop and the case particulars given to her were too vague.

Besides Hollins, who else knew that she was still interested in finding Menke's killer? Now that was an interesting question. *By going to the memorial service and passing my card around, I might as well have used a bullhorn? Did Stew's killer put her under surveillance then? Most likely. The cops and I were playing the odds that Sully would show up. Why wouldn't the real killer be there looking for Sully too? He was there, but nobody noticed him in disguise. I led them to Sully?*

This sick feeling would not go away. They were willing to kill an FBI agent, Federal security police and as many innocents to accomplish their goal. *Why did I listen to Hollins when he said very early on that the planning of the hits had a covert or military operation feel to them.* The video showed an ambush that was thwarted at the last second? Breath was hard to come by now, and her eyes watered as Marsha tried focusing on a recent Federal Employee Benefits Update on her screen. Was it time to walk away from the Menke murder? What's done is done. She can't bring him back to life. She almost got herself and Sully killed by ignoring the guidelines. *This is the reason why you don't go rogue, Marsha.*

She went over the ifs and what ifs again and again. She knew that the bomb threat was Sully's way of creating a diversion that saved their lives. She knew he would not trust her again. The video of the UPS guy showed somebody who was spooked and took the first train out of Dodge. The canvassing agents found other camera feeds of area businesses catching the UPS driver getting into a stolen van around the corner. The license plates on both of the Suburbans came back to regular cars where the owners didn't even know that their license plates had been stolen. She was tired and she tired of all of it. What did she know about running a murder investigation?

Jingles didn't bother to visit her cubicle for a parting shot. The time spent on dealing with the internal complaint forced him to work on his reports later than his regular quitting time which was ten minutes after the area supervisor in charge went home. She could set her watch by his bullshit.

Ramit walked over to her desk. "I have the items you asked me to get from the tech group."

It took so much energy to push herself out of her chair and to her feet. She followed him to the garage in a swirling fog of self-doubt and self-loathing. They stood next to her Mustang, and he activated the electronic bug locator. It looked like the remote control for a kid's race car. Sure enough, it hit on a tracker that was mounted on the right rear wheel well deep enough where the snow or slush would barely touch it. She motioned to him not to remove it. Knowing it was there was too useful now.

They walked back in silence to her cubicle. He checked her computer and her office phone for malware and listening devices with the other counter-surveillance tools. Nothing there. Lastly, he plugged a dongle into the power port of her smartphone. It was connected to a tablet-sized readout device. They watched the readout with the awful news. Her phone was compromised for both keystrokes and calls.

I told Sully to call me on this phone. Dammit. We set up the whole plan on this phone throughout several calls. Thank God he was smart enough to call from moving locations throughout the city and disconnected before anybody could get a fix.

She motioned to him to wand the conference room and then followed him.

"My car is being tracked, and my phone is being bugged. Can you fucking believe it?"

Ramit was careful with his choice of words. "The car is relatively easy to bug, but how did they get to your phone?"

"Well, I have it on my bed stand at night. I bring it into the bathroom and stream the morning news when I take a shower. It's on my desk or on me at work. Could this be done electronically or by some sort of malware?"

"Wouldn't take much for a hacker to clone it if it was on a network. When you get your coffee in the morning, do you use their WiFi?"

"Son of a bitch." She nodded.

"So they're at the coffee place, also using their WiFi. A few quick taps on an app and every text, every e-mail you typed, every keystroke and every phone call that you made went to whatever they're using to clone it. So that's another phone, or just tracking you with an app. Did you notice anything unusual?"

"My phone would fully charge overnight, and by lunchtime, it was down to almost zero. I am scheduled to have my battery replaced."

"Anything else?" he asked.

"Sometimes it would just turn off or freeze in the middle of me doing something. It was becoming annoying. I even thought about trading it in, even though it's not that old." She replied.

"Maybe you should destroy it."'

The cold hard-edged anger filled Marsha with energy. The tiredness was gone. "They came after me. They used me to get to

Sully, and it almost got us both killed. I'm gonna find out who did this and then I will use my phone for some serious proctology. I don't need an App for that."

Ramit winced.

CHAPTER THIRTY-SEVEN

Vlad purposely kept the source unaware of the operation to take out Sullivan at the Federal Courthouse. After it was aborted, he texted him in code to find out what the source could discover about the investigation into the bomb threat. He told Vlad of some of the videos from the various internal and external feeds. All the findings, the source said could not be discussed over the phone.

It resulted in a rare face to face the following day. They met on the boardwalk, adjacent to the first Atlantic City casino hotel overlooking the ocean, on a brilliantly sunny day. This was Vlad's latest daily rental. He surprised the source by bringing him to his room. Vlad's arm had healed well enough for a little R & R, and the room still smelled of sex.

The source flipped over pictures of Vlad's team from inside the courthouse lobby. "These guys are persons of interest in the bomb threat. These photos were taken after the alarms were sounded."

"They are on their way out of the country," Vlad replied. After a drive to Miami, they would charter a boat to Haiti and then a flight for Venezuela before heading back to Europe as planned.

"The license plates on these two Chevy Suburbans don't match the make and models. The owners of the cars they belonged to didn't even know they were taken off their cars. My counterparts think that both Suburbans are the kind used by executive protection companies and our own Secret Service." He turned those photos over as well on the coffee table.

"They will be difficult to replace." Vlad sighed while delivering his lie.

"What about these men?" The source played 6-second videos on his smartphone several times.

Vlad figured correctly that the two others seen running back from look-out posts to the SUVs could stay in the States, but to be safe, they were driving to Chicago where they could disappear in the sizeable Slavic population there. "They are taking a short vacation from their duties." Vlad shrugged.

"Let's talk about Sullivan now, Vlad. How did he get out of the trap you set?"

Vlad was uncomfortable with this question. "He had to have had help. He didn't like the setup and fled at the last moment."

The source laid out the best pictures of the UPS driver waiting in the building and later getting into the stolen van. He dropped the best photos of the box van driver on the table for Vlad to study. "Do you recognize either of these guys?"

None of the pictures gave Vlad a clue. "Who would be willing to risk their lives on this fool's errand? The driver couldn't be hired—Sullivan has no money. He must be Sullivan's friend. Those disguises were meant to fool me." The realization that Sullivan had assistance confirmed some of Vlad's thinking on how Sullivan was able to escape.

"It's obvious that somebody is bankrolling these disguises and transportation. Those fireworks weren't cheap either. The secret is no longer contained to just Sullivan. You have to reassess this situation, given that Sullivan had help and made a move to turn himself in," the source said.

"Would this be the right time to plan your escape? You have control of the situation if you walk away now," the source asked.

"My plans with all the Philadelphia families have not changed. While I appreciate your concern for my safety, I am relying on you to give me advanced warning. You must understand that when I take over, minor setbacks such as these are part of what I must deal with." Vlad paused. "Sullivan will not be a problem much longer." He added.

"You have brought a great deal of heat on yourself with the plan to go into a federal courthouse, guns blazing. How would it look that a man looking to turn himself in was gunned down just short of his goal? Wouldn't that cause people to look closer at Menke's murder?"

"You said your employer wants to close the Menke murder investigation. Sullivan's death would remove the problem of a messy trial."

Vlad was surprised by the source's next statement. "Suppose other bombings followed this bomb threat? Would that help you?"

"I'm listening."

"We've been keeping tabs on Dagestani students with questionable social media posts. They are generally harmless as they do not want to have to have their student visas revoked. They live mostly off the University of Penn campus." The source showed him the knot of apartments. "The Mosque is over here. The Imam is publicly neutral, but we've had a couple of plants tell us that he can get quite inflammatory in small groups."

"Islamic militants in Dagestan are fighting to establish an Islamic Caliphate across the North Caucasus. I like it. Just dropping that rumor in the media will cause a feeding frenzy." Vlad nodded his head in agreement.

"Public transportation targets would make the biggest splash.

You plant the bombs, and I will handle the evidence. We move the heat from you to the Dagestanis." The source produced a handful of college ID photos and placed them next to the surveillance photos of Vlad's men. "This is the best I could do."

Vlad nodded. "They look close enough. Are they clean-shaven now?"

"Hard to say, I can't authorize any manpower now to put them under surveillance and then act like we discovered their plan after the fact."

Vlad studied the photos and maps. His source had taken the initiative to come up with this plan. It would suck up much of the Homeland Security resources and possibly take the heat off of the recent focus on organized crime. These bold acts would bleed some assets from the federal and local agencies looking at all the mob killings in the last six weeks. This was a good plan to buy him time.

"What about the memorial service?" the source asked, bringing Vlad back to the present.

"I have to assume he was there in disguise, too, and must have recognized one of my men when he walked into the courthouse. He has employed counter-surveillance measures before, you know." Vlad rolled up his sleeve to display the nasty burns. "We both have underestimated him."

The source said, "We've had the AA meetings under video surveillance. The VA out-patient offices haven't seen him, neither has the halfway house. We put cameras on his families' houses, and the driver or Sullivan isn't in any of the feeds. We have to assume the UPS guy was Sullivan and got spooked. He left his load in the lobby and called in the bomb threat. The bomb squad said that they had a helluva time figuring out that the packages were not explosives. The boxes were filled with lots of odd-shaped metal and circuit boards."

"He knows I am trying to kill him. He knows what I look

like. He has what I want. He knows what I did to at least one person who had the video. He can't go to the police. He doesn't have many options, yet he finds ways to thwart our plans. Someone with means has taken him in. He's not out in the cold. He's not eating at the soup kitchens or in church basements." Vlad said.

"And he has at least one friend, and he is most likely still around town." The source finished Vlad's train of thought. "But there is one thing that still bothers me. Nobody in the federal government knew that Sullivan was going to turn himself in. The Bureau of Prisons had no requests. The federal marshals handle protective custody applications, and they had nothing on him. I find it hard to believe that he went to that much precaution to turn himself in cold. How did you know that he would there at that time?"

"Do you think that you are the only source I have, my friend?" Vlad smiled.

The source was about to ask another question, but Vlad interrupted him. "It is not for you to know all my secrets. You have done excellent work here and have come up with an excellent plan." He knocked on the door to the adjoining suite and said, "I am going to the steam room." The door opened to a barefoot not-so-sweet young thing wearing sheer lingerie in a cold room. Vlad ushered his source into the other room and said. "A bonus, my friend."

The grainy camera feeds all showed that it happened between 1:38 a.m. and 1:41 a.m. The footage of three bombs going off simultaneously in different parts of the city's transportation grid was similar. The train, bus, and elevated subway platforms were all deserted. The flash, concussion and smoke whited out the area under camera surveillance. All the bombs were placed just off camera.

Nearby ATMs, retail or commercial CCTV cameras caught the plumes of smoke billowing out of the enclosures. The reporters all confirmed no deaths and that only a maintenance worker, running from a scene, had a minor heart attack and survived.

Sully and Arkady surfed channels between CNN, BBC, Al Jazeera, and the local affiliates after the attacks. Cameras farther away from the hubs at ATMs showed the same single hooded figure wearing a backpack over a parka.

"This has Balderis all over it," Sully concluded.

Both men had studied his tactics since the gentlemen's club executions. The misdirection was apparent in some of the mob hits if one knew what to look for. The question puzzling them both was why? Why bring more heat on yourself?

"His people were exposed during the bomb threat. The investigation at the federal courthouse probably caught them on tape acting squirrelly." Sully added.

Arkady said, "I haven't seen my bodyguard since that night. Vlad has been off the grid. None of us want to talk to him anyway."

"How does this change our plans?" Sully asked as they watched the repeats on Fox News.

CHAPTER THIRTY-EIGHT

I t may have looked foolish to the men assembled in the upper
room of the Harbison Ave. Sports Bar and Grille, but Vlad
didn't care. The remaining capos were met by Vlad's last bodyguard, who turned on the laptop and executed the Skype
command. Vlad appeared on the screen with the bodyguard
guarding the computer. Boris from Atlantic City was in atten-
dance with the capos.

"As you know, business has proceeded without interruption.
We have continued to extend our reach with Boris giving us
excellent returns on the bars and clubs here and in South Jersey.
We are finding out that poor Yuri was helping himself to some of
the cash flow. I'm sure the Old Man allowed some of this and the
accountant probably didn't care."

Arkady interrupted. "I'm sure that accountant's dreams of
Belize were distracting."

Vlad let that one pass. "Your expanded profits have more than
covered your increase in protection payments."

It was Leonid's turn. "Speaking of which, where is this
protection you speak of? How long has it been since we've had
the company of one of your bodyguards?"

"They are working on a special operation that will bring us even greater wealth," Vlad lied. "Each one of you has more profits since the Old Man's passing, and now I am announcing that our business will grow exponentially. I will lead us into the new era. My team will end the bloodshed that has plagued all the groups since his death. We will reset the terms of protection and solidify our hold on Cyber-Fraud.

"The Cryptocurrency explosion is to us what Prohibition was to all the old school groups a century ago. The money is staggering. It makes the take from cocaine and heroin minuscule in comparison. Our reach will be global. What I am proposing is providing protection for the local groups with new and better terms for us. They will agree because their forces have been weakened by the bloodshed and retaliation. We will offer their parent groups a carrot with a small percentage of the cyberfraud in exchange for exclusivity. Everybody wins."

The capo handling identity theft began to object, but Vlad shut him down. "Don't think that credit card fraud and gas pump skimmers are in the same league as this proposal. Governments don't want to lose their stranglehold on currency. The banking industry is going the way of dinosaurs, but they don't know it yet. The most powerful forces on the planet do not want to see Cryptocurrency succeed. It is in this arena, we will rise as the supreme conquerors."

Vlad could tell they were stunned at his gambit. He saw elderly and tired twentieth-century men lacking the vision and energy that the Old Man had when he was fighting the Nazis. Vlad was not unlike the Old Man when the Old Man wore a younger man's clothes. He copied a page from the Old Man's playbook in this rise to fame. It didn't matter that he didn't know a blockchain from a blockhouse. It sounded believable. Especially when you dangle trillions of dollars as bait.

His connections to Russian special forces and clandestine

operators helped veil his plan in a cloak of mysterious possibilities. Crypto was the sugar coating on the pill of the higher cost of protection he was peddling to his own group. They didn't really have a choice, did they? No question who killed Yury and the accountant now. They were alive and making more money monthly than any month in the previous ten years.

His man and Boris exited the group with the laptop, leaving the others to mutter and wonder.

He was just minutes away from a sit-down with the Sicilians. This trial balloon was a success. He knew that the South Philly contingent would also balk at his proposal. He even knew that his new crew being assembled in Odessa would become the front-line defense for the Sicilians. The bikers would still be the outward-facing muscle and leg-breakers, but the real work would be done by his hand-picked crew.

Combining intelligence with the deeper penetration of the area's police departments and Federal agencies would keep him one step ahead of the authorities and demonstrate his willingness to prove his concept of enhanced protection for the higher fee. Applying technology and old-fashioned bribery along with military-precision small-unit operations would be his unique selling position. Then the Columbians would want his expertise, next the Dominicans and finally the Jamaicans would acquiesce. The Chinese would be guaranteed no interference. The Irish, Gypsies and independents would fall into line, too, or face the wrath of Bad Vlad. Yes, I have come to embrace my wrong side. The Old Man will be replaced by Bad Vlad, the way it is supposed to be.

This meeting with the Sicilians was not without risk. After all, he had framed one of their shooters and blew up their consigliere and that man's driver. If they suspected anything, they would dump his carcass in the swamps by the airport or take him out to the Pine Barrens. They would pat him down for a wire and weapons, but wouldn't find the GPS in his coat that, when double-clicked, would send out a 9-1-1 signal. His source had a surveillance team who wouldn't question him on stand-by. Vlad would only need to stay alive long enough to double click and pray for time.

He received the text message to drive by the Melrose Diner at Snyder and Passyunk in South Philly and head east on Snyder to the River. The surveillance teams would stay on parallel roads and not cross his path. Two dark-tinted sedans fell in behind him, and one popped out in from of him as the parade headed to the Delaware. They all came to a stop in the deserted pier facing the SS *United States*, an aging ocean liner, not quite in mothballs.

He exited his Suburban and with open hands stood in the middle of the triangle formed by the three cars. He recognized two of the drivers from the Old Man's wake. Pleasantries and high-end vodka then didn't count for anything now, as he was patted down and invited into the rear of the black Cadillac sedan.

"Thank you for meeting with me today. My condolences to you for the loss of your man and his driver."

The Boss nodded. His bodyguard side-cracked. "Fucking Columbians."

Vlad nodded in return and breathed easier. "They probably are behind the murder of our Yury and the Jamaicans that were pinned on your soldier, Mr. Falcone."

All the men in the car nodded now. The Boss spoke next. "The Old Man had a way of keeping the children from squabbling, didn't he?"

"He brought me from the old country to learn his ways. I regret not having more time with him," Vlad deadpanned. "We have been able to protect our own since then and demonstrated that we had no intention of striking out against our long-time friends and allies. It was apparent that some hot head wanted us to start fighting."

"A jackal nipping at a pride of lions," The Boss concluded. "I want to hear more of your proposal, Mr. Balderis."

"Please. Call me Vlad, sir."

"Vlad, tell me more."

Vlad detailed the plan to the Boss. The others remained silent during his pitch.

"It's all very interesting with the promises of riches from bitcoins and blockchains, but many moving parts have to fall exactly in place. I do understand that we would get a piece of the action in exchange for us not meddling in your venture. We wish you well in your new endeavor. I will talk to who I have to before I can give you what you desire." He paused.

Vlad knew the Boss had a seat on the Commission.

"Now for the immediate matters, just like the Old Man many years ago, you must prove yourself to us. Your terms are reasonable given our situations. The Old Man brought an end to the turf battles with a unique combination of reason and ruthlessness. We have all profited from the quiet. Of course, it didn't hurt that our nemesis, the FBI, became the lead dog in the domestic war on terror."

"Tell me what can I do to renew our relationship."

"The head of the man who killed my most trusted advisor and his driver. Bring it to me."

"Consider it done," Vlad said. Thinking the meeting was over Vlad pulled the door handle, it was locked. The Boss reached for his Vlad's arm and with a vise-like grip that got Vlad's attention sending shockwaves through his nervous system.

The Boss looked Vlad dead in the eye. "When you bring me his head, I want it cleaned off. Wrap it in a towel." With that said, the Boss relaxed his grip, nodded to the driver and the passenger door lock clicked open allowing Vlad to exit the car and breathe out.

He breathed deeply as the other cars left him alone on the

docks. He walked on shaky legs back to his Suburban as the wind off the river blasted him off balance. He paused to text a code to his source and precisely one minute later texted it again. He stood there and watched barges pushed by tugboats ply their trade on the river past the silent ocean liner with the darkened interior, eerily similar to the hearts of the men who drove away.

It was early morning, and the gentlemen's club was dead after doing a brisk weeknight business many hours after the Skype meeting broke up. No cover and five-dollar pitchers always attracted the locals. All the foot traffic in the area ceased. The girls, bar staff and bikers had locked up at 2 a.m. and were gone. Sully waited another hour before collapsing the bipod on his scoped hunting rifle and put everything back into the case and rucksack before walking down three flights of back stairs in the vacant commercial building 200 yards away from the club and into Arkady's waiting Mercedes SUV.

He rubbed his hands for warmth and accepted the cup of coffee savoring the first sip.

"So much for Plan B," Arkady said, as they pulled away from the alley of the neighboring street.

CHAPTER THIRTY-NINE

"Howzitgoin', Mike? Marsha asked.

"It's going, Marsha. How 'bout you?" Hollins replied.

"Another day in paradise," she answered.

The stand-up joint at Tenth and Oregon in walking distance of the baseball and football stadiums was doing a brisk lunch-time business this dry and sub-freezing late February work day. They gave their hoagie orders to the ancient man at the chest-high window over the clatter made by of an equally old short-order cook slicing and dicing sizzling sirloin on the oiled grill behind him. The locals knew that this place offered the best cheesesteaks in the city. Her father would bring her and Nick here on warm summer night ballgames at Veterans Stadium before they demolished it.

He would badge them into the 400 level seats behind home plate, and they would savor their steaks with Whiz during batting practice. Marsha looked for any excuse to relive the nostalgia of those days with her two favorite guys.

Today, Marsha took the subway and left her work phone at the office. The meeting with Mike was her idea, but she wasn't taking any chances. She wanted to trust him, but knowing that he had been in her car and spent time with her close up, she had to be extra careful.

Since the simultaneous bombings, it had been all-hands-on-deck. Even Jingles was out on the street annoying everybody. Every available agent was chasing their tails, trying to find terrorists.

All the leads on all the mob-related killings came to a stand-still. All the intelligence-gathering stopped. Terrorism was the Bureau's number one responsibility. There was no questioning that directive. With Sullivan not talking to her, she had very little to go on. Her requests for the video feed at the stores where the Temple tracksuits were sold were slowly winding their way through corporate channels. Without grand jury subpoenas all she and Ramit could do was ask and ask again.

"I'm dead in the water with finding out who killed Menke," she said between mouthfuls.

They now sat in Mike's brown beat-to-hell Ford police inter-ceptor with the sandwich paper wrappers on their laps. "Do your people have a line on Sullivan?" she asked innocently enough.

"Somebody has to be hiding him. He's in the wind," Mike said.

"You don't disappear from being homeless and living in a tent in the middle of winter without help," Marsha agreed.

"You think he's dead? Last time we talked to him, he had barely survived freezing to death," Mike posited.

"I might have said yes if he hadn't booby-trapped his tent hours before Homicide's arrest warrant was going to drop on him. He had an exit strategy. Keep in mind, he was a Scout-Sniper with the marines. The guy's been in tougher situations than this and survived. I know he's the key to everything." Marsha let that hang in the air. Let him wonder how she knew that.

"Given the fact that a crime reporter was killed, Homicide still has this as a priority case, even with all the other OC killings. Wes Montgomery is like a dog with a bone on this one. He wants Sullivan bad."

Marsha said, "I saw Montgomery at Menke's memorial service. He gave me the stink eye when I started to talk to Menke's family and friends about what Stew was working on before he died."

"Whaddya want, Marsha? You were stepping on his toes with that federal boot of yours when you started asking people there about the Mob angle. He's thinking that an FBI agent is sticking her nose where it doesn't belong. In his mind, you're creating reasonable doubt as to the motive for Menke's killing."

"Yeah, well when they catch Menke's real killer, his arrest warrant will be Exhibit A for the killer's defense. I confirmed that nobody from the PD talked to his friends. They all said he was spooked by what he was working on and was acting paranoid. So don't talk to me about stepping on toes or where my nose goes. You bailed on me, remember?" There it was, she needed him back on this case now in a big way.

"Hold your horses. I didn't bail on you. I gave you everything I had, and I got even more stuff that connects the killings between Menke and the Russian accountant."

C'mon Mike talk to me. Marsha waited and kept working bites of her hoagie around in her mouth. She didn't know which way this conversation was going, but if he were any kind of cop, he'd want to get back in the ballgame.

She saw that he wanted to tell her and was struggling with what he had and how to say it. The gamesmanship finally ended with, "We got information where the dump site might have been. It paid off. We were able to take tire impressions, and it was the unique tread of tire that can hold 'run flat' inserts used on GM Executive Protection vehicles. We narrowed the make and models to three: Yukons, Envoys or Suburbans. Our lab tested the plastic wrapper on the floater, and there were fibers from a vehicle's interior carpeting on the outside of the wrapper."

"I had two Chevy Suburbans outside the Federal Courthouse during the bomb threat."

Hollins looked confused. "Whaddya talkin' about?"

She put down her hoagie. Her appetite was gone. She wrapped it up and finished her soda before going down the road of no return.

"I was there. I had an appointment with an AUSA and was in the lobby when the bomb threat was called in. I saw a couple of no-necks who looked like they were wearing comms. They didn't budge when the alarms went off. It wasn't until all the cops and fire trucks responded did they skedaddle. I tailed them to the glass entrance and watched them beat feet into a couple black tinted-out Suburbans. I made a nuisance of myself until I could confirm what I saw on the security camera video feeds."

Mike chewed his hoagie slowly and took another bite, then sipped his soda and took another bite. He cleared his throat and asked, "How did they know Sullivan was going to be there?"

Smart guy! "Mike, I took the subway here to meet you and left my phone at my office playing Motown hits. Somebody put a GPS on my car, and my phone was cloned. I almost got me and him and a lot of other innocent people killed."

"No shit."

"Uh-huh. I was in their kill zone and was fucking clueless. Sullivan spotted them and had his buddy call in the bomb threat. He probably was no more than ten yards away from me and from walking into Federal Protective Custody. He got spooked and boogied. Good thing too. Otherwise, you'd be going to my funeral."

CHAPTER FORTY

There were a dozen martial arts studios in Center City offering Jiu-Jitsu, but only three that were exclusively Brazilian. Arkady told Sully that Vlad brought his work-out kitbag into the Old Man's hospital room. He couldn't recall the full name but was sure it was Brazilian studio.

He couldn't take a chance on an AA meeting, even out in the suburbs. The Big Book only went so far. On days like these, when he was mission-focused, his thoughts of drinking were scattered and fleeting. The sirens weren't calling him. He marveled that he had been sober for almost a month. He was putting on weight now, mostly muscle, with a steady diet of quality protein and pull-ups, chin-ups, and burpees. Wanna drink? Do burpees until exhaustion. Feel sorry for yourself? Think of what happened to Stew and how he saved your life. Wanted for a murder that you didn't commit? Focus on eliminating the threat to your own life. Sitting there with his rifle, staring out the tinted window at this studio's entrance was very peaceful. His full attention rested on the comings and goings of the mixed martial artists. Could he go one on one with Vlad, if he had to? Hopefully, it wouldn't come to that. He carried his .45 cal auto and 5011 full-size KA-BAR knife at all times.

After the courthouse fiasco, he and Arkady debated their plans again. Was he justified in defending himself from a trained killer? He would make it look like a revenge killing that was so prevalent now in the city. After all, it was Vlad who started killing organized criminals while creating the misdirection. They agreed that afterward they would drop the thumb drive in the mail to Detective Hollins. They reasoned that once Bad Vlad was no more, the police department would have no problem with clearing Stew's death.

Was he taking a chance? Absolutely. Was he taking another's life? No doubt about it. Was it murder? Yep. Cold-blooded? Absolutely. Was he revenging the death of his only friend? Completely. Would he be able to sleep at night? Like a baby.

Vlad would have shot up a federal courthouse entrance to kill him. He reminded himself that he had killed, in the sandbox, under sometimes questionable circumstances. Like the time he zeroed in on the IED being carried by a kid intending to put it under an approaching convoy. At 400 yards, the shot ignited the bomb and vaporized the kid. And what about that time he called in an airstrike on a rebel stronghold where they didn't think that the Americans would drop ordinance on them because of possible non-combatants clustered in the surrounding buildings. He could think of a half-dozen gray-area shots that were his call back then. Those were the ones and the deaths of his friends that chewed away on his sanity. Taking one more bad guy out would not be a problem.

He didn't ask for this. He didn't want it to come to this. He went to his government, and they couldn't protect him. Thinking back to that day, O'Shea would have died too along with many others. She was not in on the plot to kill him, he was sure. Somebody found out, somehow, and he was lucky that Arkady spotted one of Vlad's goons just in the nick of time.

Was his target playing it safe with the Skype meeting? *Was Balderis staying away from the Russians until the thorn in his side was permanently removed?* Regardless of his speculation, it felt good to be the silent hunter again. *Was he a killer?* Professionally trained by the marines to do his duty? Yes. *Assassin?* No. *Did he like killing?* Not really.

Coming back from Afghanistan, it only took one time in the Poconos hunting whitetail deer to convince him otherwise. He had put the crosshairs on an Eight point just after dawn one cold rainy late November morning, and he paused. He shifted the scope from center mass to the deer's eyes and saw a creature that didn't need to die for someone's sporting pleasure. He walked out of the woods loud enough to send the big guy crashing through the laurel and over the ridgeline away from his dad and brother to live another day. On the other hand, the animal that would have gutted him like a deer while he slept in his tent or shot him up in a government building needed to be dropped like a bad habit.

It was on days like this that he felt most alive and the PTSD or alcohol didn't jangle his nerves and zombie his feet into the liquor store. Veterans didn't talk about their war experiences very often, but they almost all agreed that they felt the most alive when they were surrounded by death.

He watched the comings and goings. He knew he would have no problem recognizing his prey if he appeared. He knew what to do.

CHAPTER FORTY-ONE

"When Mike Hollins started making noise that he wanted me to get the tapes from the Bureau on the bomb threat, I didn't think much of it. After all, he would come to me at the Fusion Center for that sort of stuff."

Nick said to his father, the retired captain of the vice unit, "It seemed odd that a guy in the Organized Crime squad would want them. Some bullshit about a witness to the organized crime hit at a gentlemen's club in the Northeast who was trying to get into the Witness Protection Program."

Marsha was getting uncomfortable with where this was headed. Nick hadn't talked to her recently about the OC connection to Menke's murder and thought that he was pre-occupied with the bombings that had consumed the city and much of the nation in a belief that terrorists were behind the explosions. Since the hand-off to Hollins, she had been on the bombings B Team running down leads and going nowhere.

"So I tell my contact with the Bureau that Hollins is working an OC angle, and they look at me like I have two heads, but since I know how to play nice, they give me the tapes and who do I see standing there, looking around cool as a cucumber, while all hell is breaking out and people are fleeing the building." Nick laid the 8 x 10 on the dining room table for his father and Marsha to see.

"This always happens. I look ten years older and twenty pounds heavier in surveillance videos," she said.

"What's this about?" her father asked, alarmed by the connection.

Sunday dinner was still about fifteen minutes away, and her mother knew how to keep busy in the kitchen during tense conversations like these.

"What's the big deal? When I was 1500 miles away runnin' and gunnin' with the cartels, we mixed it up pretty good down there. You weren't all up in my business." She tried deflecting the obvious.

"Yeah and I worried about you every day," Drummond Sr. said.

"Me too, Sis," Nick added.

"Is this where I get reminded that everybody wished I had become a high school Phys. Ed teacher and volleyball coach?" Maybe Marsha could still turn this around long enough until she went into the kitchen to help mom with the pot roast.

"This is about you not telling anybody the play that you were going to run. No back-up, no plan, just winging it. Down there you were part of a team. Everybody had everybody's back. Since when did you decide to be a cowboy?" Nick was blunt.

The Drummond men were team players. Being called a cowboy was the worse insult that Nick had thrown at her since they were teenagers. "Okay, I admit it. I called my own number. I wasn't playing with the other boys and girls who have badges and guns. I got into something that I shouldn't have. Excuse me for thinking that a cold meet in a federal courthouse could go sideways."

"I don't even wanna know what you were doin' there. Just tell me that you are done with it." Nick was her big brother, a leader of coppers and a seasoned investigator. He stared a hole through her.

The imploring look on her father's face was one she had never seen before. It was excruciating to see him so worried about her. They had their differences over the years, sure, but this felt different. In his face was a mix of all the hard feelings—fear, doubt, and frustration. Her understanding of her own mortality and the emotions inherent in narrowly escaping a death brought about from her actions had been weighing heavily on her as well. Did her grasp for the achievement of bringing in Sullivan, solving Menke's murder and connecting all the hits, blind her to risks that she took?

"Yeah, I'm done playin' cowboy," she said to them trailing her hand on their shoulders as she made her way towards the kitchen. "Mom, do you need some help in there?" Maybe she could take her frustration out on the mashed potatoes.

CHAPTER FORTY-TWO

The tip that a drug shipment was coming into a small suburban airfield was solid enough to roll on. The Whitpain Police, Pennsylvania State Police, and Joint Drug Task Force were all called together on this one. Wings Field, just northwest of the city, was the last place anybody expected a cocaine drop to take place. Especially in daylight. The weather this last Friday of February was mild and dry, after a brutal and unpredictable winter. A private plane chartered by a straw company used by the Columbian cartel had lifted off from a similar airport in Fort Lauderdale and was en route. It was unclear who would meet the plane and offload the shipment for their Philadelphia connection. That part was unknown, at least, to the legitimate law enforcement officials hunkered down at the police station in Blue Bell making their plans for the takedown.

Vlad and his source knew who was coming to make the pickup. Fresh bodies and guns were winging their way northward; the cocaine was added to the flight because that's what you do when you run a drug cartel.

Vlad's plan was simple enough. The execution relied on

everybody in this production sticking to the script. Good guys acting like good guys, bad guys acting like bad guys and Vlad being Bad Vlad.

He watched through his camera's telescopic lens as the stealthy SWAT teams made their way to rooftops and observation posts. The Mobile Command Center retired to the backside of a nearby office park. Unmarked chase vehicles were positioned behind other buildings near the field.

It was a work day, and traffic reflected the comings and goings of delivery trucks, tradesmen and mid-day errand-runners. It was too early for school to be letting out. The airport's recreational flyers were politely but firmly told to go home. If the Columbians had the scene under surveillance, the plane would have veered off course by now and would be making an unplanned landing at any of the dozen putt-putt airstrips with no flight towers in the Delaware Valley. That didn't seem to be the case, as it vectored past Dover AFB and Wilmington Delaware into Pennsylvania. This twin turbo-prop could land on less than 2500 feet of hardtop. Vlad assumed that once the plane was on the ground, the police would direct the tower to keep other planes circling until the takedown was completed and the scene secured.

He observed two stretch limousines pull into the airfield. They drove straight to the striped-off waiting area. The plane would taxi to them, and since this was a small regional airport, the flight would disgorge its occupants from a stairway right to the tarmac. No TSA here. All the SWAT people were tucked away now, and the waiting game began in earnest.

This was what he lived for. He had good intel. He had the proper equipment. He had an excellent spot to watch from. He had good comms. It is was in this moment he felt his destiny would be secured as a major player in this town. This operation would secure his position with both the Sicilians and the unwitting Columbians. He knew that the Dominicans and Jamaicans would fall in line for Bad Vlad's protection, once a truce was affected between the two larger groups.

The plane came in from the south and circled the field once before banking for the FAA mandated counter-clockwise approach into the wind. It landed uneventfully and taxied to the drop-off.

Vlad readied his camera to focus wide enough to include both limos in his viewfinder.

When the occupants of the plane were half-way between what brought them to the horse country outside of Philadelphia and what would take them to their new hunting ground, the cops sprang into action.

From innocent looking service trucks, black-clad men with Kevlar helmets and short-barreled machine guns intercepted the half-dozen men who were weighed down with large duffel bags. The bags went straight to the ground as their hands went straight to their heads. They were then planted face-down on the ground.

At the same time, SWAT vehicles raced in from the nearby hangars and boxed in the stretch limos. More SWAT team members pulled on the doors of the limos and extricated the occupants.

Vlad identified the Columbian's leader on his comm set before the head honcho went down to the ground. Vlad pressed record on his camera and began taking in the scene and slowly focused on Numero Uno.

When that man was finally hoisted to his feet and steadied, his head exploded like a pumpkin with a large firecracker inside. His blood and brains saturated the face shield of the SWAT man holding the now lifeless body.

Vlad's sniper left his NATO-approved rifle with a silencer in his sniper hide and rolled down the hill to his motorcycle hidden in the brush and rode the speed limit to the rally point. Vlad moved to the driver's seat of his vehicle in a nearby corporate park and did the same.

I didn't have a towel, so hopefully, this will do. Vlad thought.

CHAPTER FORTY-THREE

"Where's Ray?" Joe asked. He was dressed in his Center City businessman attire and was staring at an unfamiliar face.

"Who's asking?" came the reply from the man taking out the trash in the back of the Unitarian Church near Temple University. He appeared wary of this well-dressed man carrying two empty banker's boxes.

"Ray would let my step-brother Joe keep his stuff here when he was homeless. He asked me to box it up and send it to him in Arizona." Joe responded without answering.

"Joe who?" the man asked.

Too many questions. Joe thought. "My brother told me where they stashed it and I can show you."

"Wait here until I can get somebody to okay this." The man pulled the service door closed.

Joe stood with his coat lapels up, and his hat pulled down to ward off the eyes of the camera over the back door. Even this building needed security cameras in this part of town.

The temperature was mild for late February and dry for a change. There was no breeze to speak of and dusk was settling in.

Several minutes went by. Joe was getting itchy. Eventually, the door opened.

A different man opened the door. "How can I help you?"

Joe repeated his spiel.

"Do you have some ID?" He was taller, younger and was dressed in a brown warm turtle-neck sweater over matching corduroys.

Joe reached into his coat pocket, produced a beautiful leather wallet filled with a whole new identity and held out his driver's license: William Ratcliffe with a Society Hill row house address. Joe held onto the card while the man inspected it in a little tug of war. Finally, the man let go and said, "Follow me."

Joe went down the familiar hallway, but the man made a left at the next hallway and not to the right where Joe's belongings had been kept. Joe stopped at the intersection. The man, who had taken out the trash, stopped short behind him and between Joe and the back door. The leader turned back and cordially said, "We had to move some things around for the upcoming repairs to the meeting rooms."

The procession proceeded down yet another hall to what appeared to be this administrator's office given that his family photo appeared on the modest desk next to the phone. The man reached for his key ring.

"Which one is it?" Slowly, he tried different keys in the storage closet lock. Then he dropped them and started over. Joe noticed the man's hand was trembling. He looked back at the face of Ray's replacement and made out a similar sense of alarm. Just as Joe was about to bolt, the door opened, and the outside light switch illuminated his belongings stuffed in the furthest corner of the room. Joe breathed a little easier and went into the room and bent down to begin grabbing the things that mattered most to him when he had to leave his family under the watchful eye of the Bensalem Police. He was elbows deep in the old crate that held his prize possessions when the room went dark, and the door closed with a whoosh and click.

"Hey, what's going on?" The men on the other side were holding the doorknob.

"The police will be here any minute. You can explain it to them," came the shrill response from the administrator.

Joe relaxed his grip on the knob and tried jerking it open. He felt their resistance on the other side.

Using the light from his cell phone he reached for his multi-purpose tool and began unscrewing the screws holding the doorknob in place. He was able to do so in less than two minutes, and the knobs fell off. The light from the room was welcome, but he found the room empty. He ran to the office door and pulled on the doorknob. It moved, but the deadbolt held the door shut.

Immediately he heard from the hallway, "Police!"

Joe ran back into the storage room, pulled out his brother's birthday present again and began puncturing the drywall. He expanded the perforations into a hole that allowed him to kick out a section between the metal studs set two feet on center. The drywall on the other side gave way, and he stumbled into an adjacent room. The elderly women clutching their book of the month were standing, mouths agape at the intruder who just burst through the wall.

He ran past them and into another hallway that led to the large congregation meeting room. He reached the fire exit at the back of the building and hit the door at the same time another police officer was opening it. Joe lowered his shoulder like a running back and knocked the officer over and sent the cop's firearm flying.

Joe was sprinting between the side by side recycle and garbage dumpsters. He went back through the hole in the fence. Not having forgotten the alleys and walkways where he had passed out or staggered piss-drunk less than a month earlier, Joe ran the obstacle course like he was back at Parris Island. He heard sirens closing in from all directions. He had one chance to escape and knew what to do.

The Broad Street Car Wash was going to be open for another hour. It was two blocks away. When he burst out of an alley and waited for a police car to pass on Broad Street. He saw that the car towel-dry and vacuum station was empty now as the skeleton crew was hunkered down in the shack next to the car wash exit keeping warm and listening to music. The automatic car wash wasn't being used at the moment. Joe slipped into the room where the dryers were spinning towels.

He had unsuccessfully worked there the previous fall, and he knew he could hide behind the mechanicals until they closed. He drank and passed out there the night that he got his one and only paycheck.

CHAPTER FORTY-FOUR

*H*ow *many times has this guy gotten away?* The source complained to himself. Between Afghanistan and here, how many times has this jarhead gotten a pass? He is human and had a soft place. Going back for his stuff at the church was weak and stupid. Did he think that nobody there would alert us that the belongings of a suspected killer were taking up space in their building? It was a good thing that the regular janitor was sick with the flu. How can you blame the first uniforms in for wanting to nab a killer?

The sick feeling in his stomach was growing. Every day this guy is loose, is another day that the secrets could get out. *Can I live without the bribe money? Sure. Could I live with the fact that 30 years of bribes would be exposed? Unacceptable.*

My fly-bag is ready too. Uruguay is beautiful this time of year. Plenty of willing young things to occupy my time. But what about the others? Some of the guys would have to stay and take the fall. I can't let that happen.

Walking the tightrope between duty and dishonor was becoming more difficult for the source. He thought about those high-wire guys that could walk the tightrope for years, and one day, a fluke gust of wind comes up, and they become an exciting splat video on a Facebook feed. His reasons to stick around now had grown exponentially, but only one other person knew why. With Sullivan having an accomplice, it was just a matter of time before the shit would hit the fan. He had to hope for a twofer.

The Licensing and Inspections guy will find the bomb-making materials in the Dagestanis' apartment basement tomorrow morning. *This will buy us more time and close the loop on that misdirection. How much longer could we hope to hold out?*

What was becoming more apparent to the source now was that neutralizing Vlad would maybe reduce the outcomes that were more important to him. Sullivan would still need to play the video to start the process of trying to exonerate himself in Stew Menke's murder. Would he need to give over the spreadsheets? The PD would suffer a black eye for wanting the wrong guy, but that was the least of his worries. *It wasn't the first time we got the wrong guy, and it wouldn't be the last.*

CHAPTER FORTY-FIVE

Along with the stunning news of the arrests of the Dagestanis for the transportation bombings that first Tuesday of March, a fresh, clean breeze swept through the Delaware Valley hinting at a mild dry spell. The mid-40s temps teased Marsha with the promise of an early spring.

She desperately needed a change. Maybe this was a good omen. She couldn't remember a worse winter of weather and discontent in her lifetime. The mob hits and Menke's unsolved murder weighed on her as much as the snafu at the courthouse, leaving her feeling impotent in all things investigative.

There she sat, doing what did second best. Jingles had tasked her to work the money trail on the Columbian cartel. Their leadership was decimated following the takedown at Wings Field. The sniper rifle found at the scene left no clues as to the culprit, save the brass. Every SWAT member was swabbed for powder residue just to rule out any trigger-happy good guy wearing black. The high-velocity round left enough fragments to tie it back to the gun, but the shooter left nothing of evidentiary value behind.

As for the rest of the cartel members, getting true identities on the plane's passenger and the car's passengers were given to other team members.

Her job was to find out who rented the limos. She also had all the arrestee's wallets and was elbows deep in tracing their credit cards. The forged driver's licenses and passports were put on Amtrak with an intern to give to the Documents people in DC.

Working financial crimes with her Accounting degree from Penn State and CPA had its advantage. She joined the Bureau at the advent of the internet's commercial possibilities and used her knowledge to track down fugitives and robbery suspects. Microchips and shoe leather, she liked to say. It was a never-ending game of chess. Sometimes, she was a move ahead, but most times law enforcement was a step behind. That was the case until domestic terrorism deterrence began evening the playing field. Data mining and link analysis tools used to uncover threats could be adapted to the cartels and other international groups.

With everything scanned into an OCR spreadsheet and with all her queries out to the credit granting institutions, she still had to drive out to the limo rental location. Wonders never ceased, a pool car was available. She grabbed the keys and started towards the elevator but turned on her heel and walked back to Ramit's tech grotto.

"Hey, Ramit." He was so engrossed in what was happening on his two monitors that he was genuinely startled and jumped up. Unfortunately, he was still tethered to his headphone and pulled his laptop into the ergonomic keyboard pushing it off the table which then dragged the laptop to the floor.

"Oh, hi, Marsha," Ramit said with headphones in one hand and a keyboard in the other.

"I see you have your hands full," Marsha said with a wry smile thinking, I still like getting a rise out of young men once in a while.

He set everything back and was still blushing. "What's up?"

"I owe you a little dinner and field trip. Can you spare a couple of hours?"

Torn between leaving his desk a mess or going with Marsha, Ramit hesitated for only a brief moment and said, "Let's go."

They chatted about everything but the Menke murder on their way out to the rental place. Both of them stared at her cell phone on the dashboard like it was poison. The sun was shining, not a cloud in the sky. For the first time this winter, they could run the heater on low and pull in fresh air through the vents. They people-watched the swarms of pedestrians out shaking off cabin-fever.

"The clientele of this establishment appreciates their privacy," the limo man said. He was nattily dressed in an English-tailored charcoal gray suit. The dark tie over a starched button-down collar white shirt touched the top of his thin belt. It all matched his Italian dress shoes which had never stepped in a slush pile. The equally well-dressed eye candy who served as the desk receptionist stood behind him with a similarly disdainful scowl, after having been badged and berated by Marsha to go fetch the boss.

"So you have no cameras?" Marsha confirmed.

"That is correct," Smug Man replied.

"Applications and photo ID, please."

"I will take your request under advisement—" looking at her business card, "Special Agent O'Shea." He didn't move.

Marsha looked at Ramit, then to the receptionist and finally back to the owner.

"Let me understand this. The government has impounded your two limos worth about a hundred Gs a piece. Their return is questionable, given that they were to be used to transport drugs, guns, and illegals by a drug cartel."

"The guns, drugs and illegals were not in the cars, as I understand," the perfectly coiffed and manicured man volleyed back.

"Without showing me the customers' rental agreements, I have to proceed with the belief that you were an accessory to the conspiracy to transport drugs, guns and illegals to a felony murder." Marsha ratcheted up the conversation by tossing her handcuffs to Ramit who fumbled the catch and bobbled them in the air like a third-string slot receiver before clutching them to his chest.

Mouths and eyes wide open, the receptionist and Ramit watched as the man replied without breaking eye contact.

"This isn't the first time, how do you say it, Agent O'Shea, that I have been to the rodeo. Please send a subpoena to this attorney. Your organization already knows my name and the name of the company I am subcontracted by appears nowhere on the title, registration or insurance policies of the vehicles in question. We simply expedite their rentals for a commission."

He reached into his coat pocket removed an exquisite tan leather billfold, extracted a crisp, clean business card of a high-powered white-collar crime attorney who Marsha knew ten years earlier had been a hard-charging assistant United States attorney. "But, you already knew that, Agent O'Shea."

"And here, I was hoping to expedite the return of your expensive cars in exchange for your cooperation. Oh well. I am sorry to have troubled you." She smiled tightly, and Ramit barely caught up with her as they exited the establishment next.

Marsha took in a deep breath looked at the clear blue sky, listened to the sound traffic buzzing by on Cheltenham Avenue and slowly exhaled. "Kenny said it best Ramit."

"Kenny?"

"You have to know when to hold them, know when to fold them, know when to walk away and know when to run, Ramit."

She found a country station on the radio and began singing along with the chorus for the benefit of her listener to as many songs as she could stand. They drifted south down Broad Street back towards Center City and their offices, but in North Philly, she turned at Temple University towards Stew Menke's apartment. They stopped and stared. Nothing was said while the music droned on. *What am I doing here? I'm finished with this case.* Darkness descended on Marsha's thought this pre-Spring day. *What is this scene trying to tell me? Stew talk to me. I am listening now.*

There was a couple of drunks standing across the street from the liquor store. Several male students approached them. Marsha and Ramit watched them talk. The boys reached into their pockets, and one then handed the drunk the wad of collected cash. He almost got clipped by a car in his hurry to cross the street and go inside the store. He returned with a couple of bags and a shorty. The boys looked in the bags, slapped him on the shoulder and departed. He walked in the opposite direction with his shorty. Marsha pointed out to Ramit the next group of students who approached the next drunk and the scene repeated itself.

Marsha stuffed her phone into the console and motioned to Ramit to exit the car. They walked over to the liquor store and saw the cameras covering the whole sidewalk and the foyer from three separate cameras.

The cashier was behind the counter. Marsha badged him and said, "We want your film from your outside cameras." She gave him the times and date.

"I'm sorry. I just started working here, and the manager won't be back until closing time. I don't know how to work the system."

"That's okay, I do," Ramit said. "My name is Ramit Ravicant, I am an FBI electronics technician. Take me back to the security set up. My associate here will watch the front door for you."

Marsha stood there like a good soldier and nodded.

Five minutes became ten and then twenty. Marsha told the drunks to come back later.

Ramit and the clerk returned. Ramit shook his smartphone and jangled a thumb drive from his key ring at Marsha. "Got it. If the cops looked at it, they would have been off by an hour. This system is still on Daylight Savings Time."

"No one came in," Marsha duly reported.

Ramit reached for the clerk's hand. "Thanks a lot, Percy, I appreciate it. I'll put in a good word with the Director when your application comes in."

Marsha did her best to keep a straight face.

Outside in the daylight, he shielded his phone from the sun, and she craned over his neck, careful not to stick a boob in his back. They watched it once.

"The time was off by an hour," Ramit pointed out.

They watched as Sullivan came up to the entrance from the direction of Stew's apartment and started to go into the store and stopped. Sullivan hesitated and walked away from the door and away from Stew's apartment. Sullivan was carrying a Trader Joe's bag.

"This was 60 minutes before the first-floor tenants heard noises and then dead silence from the third floor. Pictures don't lie, Ramit. That is Sullivan. That is the man I saw in the hospital bed almost a week later. He passed up the liquor store. He promised Stew he was going to get sober." Marsha's words gushed out.

They watched it again. Then again. The sun was starting to set, and it was getting colder by the minute, but Marsha was elated. She reached into her purse, fished out a card with Hollins' cell phone number on it.

Using Ramit's phone, she called him. "Mike, hi. It's Marsha. Yeah, this is Ramit's phone. Yes, Mike." Then to Ramit, "Mike says hi."

"Hey, Mike," Ramit said.

"Okay, get this," Marsha continued. "The liquor store is in shouting distance of Menke's apartment, and I'm watching a video of Sullivan standing in front of it and leaving the area an hour before the murder. Mike, this proves that he was telling the truth. Whoever looked at the video at the PD got the times wrong. It was still on Daylight Savings time today when we looked at it. I'll send this over to you. Call me back after you get it."

It didn't take long for Mike to call back.

Mike called back and Ramit answered. "Yes, I am positive the time on the recorder never changed. Every month from then to now, I checked for sunrise and sunset. They never changed it." Ramit listened some more and handed the phone to Marsha.

She listened. "I just gave you a fresh set of downs. Find the man with the tracksuit, and you got your killer." Marsha listened for a minute without saying anything and then said, "Goodbye, Mike. Mike says goodbye, Ramit."

"Goodbye, Mike," Ramit said.

"One more thing, Marsha. I took two pictures of this business card that was sitting by the monitor and hard drive."

She looked at it and said, "No way."

Ramit said, "Yes way."

It was her good friend Homicide Detective Wes Montgomery's card with his cell phone number inked in on the back.

They got back in the car and Ramit said, "Marsha, can you play that song from earlier?"

For the rest of the ride back to the office, Ramit and Marsha sang along with Kenny from a YouTube video.

CHAPTER FORTY-SIX

There would be no summit. Vlad shuttled between the groups and started the process of redesigning the protection agreements. All the while, he was recruiting his new team, and they would be ready to fly into Canada in a few days, cross the border and pick up their new identities in Chicago and ride back with his guys that had been cooling their heels there after the courthouse debacle. He would be stronger than ever.

He wasn't surprised that he wasn't getting more pushback from his own crime group. They witnessed what he did to the Old Man and rightly surmised how the accountant met his fate. A few grumbled about Yury's demise, but it all served to keep them in line. They got soft, and they didn't have the resolve to challenge him.

Sullivan had proven his resourcefulness in eluding the police. He had an accomplice now, but they seemed satisfied to stay in the shadows. Vlad could hope that Sullivan would make another mistake again. Was he drinking again? Would he slip up? With a little persuasion, he might learn about the accomplice and dispose of him as well.

"I orchestrated the whole operation. Anybody who might have had anything to do with the bombing of your consigliere was taken out." Vlad showed them the video of the Columbian boss losing his head in slow motion. "Their operation will not recover any time soon. They were quick to accept my offer of protection. Maybe a little too quick for I made them an outstanding offer. They refused to accept responsibility for the death of your man and used the example how your own soldier Mr. Falcone was set up."

"That is true. We knew that the killing of your lieutenant in the strip club was a set up too," The Boss pointed out.

"As did we." Vlad pointed out. "The Columbians deny any involvement there as well, but here is what I can tell you. I was able to increase the percentage of my take from them and the Jamaicans. I wanted to tell you that I will not ask for an increase from your agreement with the Old Man. The other groups must pay off the war debt. Tonight, I will approach the Dominicans, with whom we have no quarrel, but first, they must come to understand that they will stand alone against all the other groups if they don't fall in line."

Vlad stirred the espresso served to him at his host's favorite back-room meeting place. He waited for the men across from him to finish their discussion in the tongue of their Mediterranean island homeland.

"Vladislav, you have exceeded yourself in bringing the Columbians to their knees and making them pay for all the trouble they caused. You demonstrate the ability to speak as softly as the Old Man did, yet you also carry a bigger stick. It's time to put an end to this unnecessary bloodshed." He nodded his approval.

After the meeting, Vlad walked the short distance to his Suburban. It had been under the watchful eyes of his hosts, but also from his shadow car. He had taken to this extra precaution recently.

Robbie Mondesi's younger brother was the enforcer for Dominicans, who through unfortunate circumstance was now thrust into a leadership role as a survivor of the recent carnage. He probably was at their club the night when Vlad turned Mondesi the Older and Warren Marichal into pulpy organic wall art.

They sat now, each with a bodyguard standing behind them, in another club's back room on Kensington at Allegheny.

He just lacked the skills to negotiate. Coming from the school of hit first and talk later, this meeting was awkward for both men. Vlad talked about the fragile truce that was struck, which would allow the groups to strengthen and go back to making money instead of spending it in a war of attrition.

Cisco Mondesi just shrugged and said he didn't need any help and he didn't need to pay the Russians for protection. His crew could handle it for themselves.

Vlad talked about how his elite forces, intelligence gathering abilities and bribery reach could not only allow them to hold onto to what they had but grow their reach into the northern and southern counties with the bikers as willing partners. Cisco said that he didn't need any bikers to move his product.

Vlad spent time going over both carrots again, but Cisco was getting bored and impatient.

Here was the opportunity to play his strongest card. He motioned for his bodyguard to leave the room. He was now alone with Cisco and waited for the macho man to respond in kind. Mondesi motioned to his man to do the same. His bodyguard began to protest, but Mondesi held his hand up to signal the end of the one-sided conversation. Both men sat alone now.

"We are not the biggest fish in the pond," Vlad started. "I

made peace with the Sicilians, the Columbians, and the Jamaicans. Many have died recently, but the killing can end with a new agreement on the table. Why stand alone and risk having everyone turn against you? You have the power to take control of your organization and grow it the way you want without interference from the others. That is my guarantee."

"And why do I need you to do that for me? Why should I pay for your protection?" Mondesi replied.

Vlad nodded and reached into his pocket. He retrieved a bullet and slid it across the table. It rolled across the table until it stopped by Cisco's palm. The Dominican saw his name scratched into it.

"Cisco, I believe you can do great things here. Please let me help you. Help me keep you safe." Vlad retrieved his bullet and stood up.

Cisco nodded weakly, but he nodded just the same, and the deal was done.

Twenty minutes later, Vlad was cruising across the Ben Franklin Bridge. He was going to celebrate in Atlantic City. From the time the Old Man died until now, he had waited for this moment to arrive. He was elated. He brought the different gangs to their knees and then to the bargaining table. He hadn't felt this excited in many years, and now it was all coming to fruition. He was lucky, yes, but he could argue that he made his own luck. He turned the music up and was tapping along to the beat. Today was the best day of this whole wretched winter.

Vlad successfully navigated the confounding New Jersey highway rotary at Cherry Hill when he heard the phone ringing. Boris.

Not a phone call, a video call. Vlad thumbed the screen on.

"Boris, what is wrong? What is wrong with you?"

Slowly Boris' bound and gagged face was pushed out of the

frame. Arkady's face now filled the screen, and he said, "Good evening, Vlad. I hope you are having a nice evening. Boris is my guest for the moment. I want to be clear with you. Sullivan is dead. He drank himself to death. I have the video feed from the gentlemen's club. I am in charge now. I will contact you again this way with instructions on when and where I will meet you."

CHAPTER FORTY-SEVEN

Wes Montgomery wanted to kill her. Marsha wasn't sure yet whether it was figuratively or literally. Finding his business card and the video of Sully leaving the area of Stew's apartment an hour before the murder, made him look either stupid for not knowing that the cameras were off by an hour or tunnel-visioned because he had already decided that Sullivan was the guy. His hot temper exploded when he found out his favorite FBI agent, who had been removed from the case, discovered the video.

Hollins told her that Montgomery made up a weak-ass excuse that he left his business card there and never bothered to follow up to retrieve the video after Sullivan's prints came back on the murder weapon.

It was 4:30 by the time word had traveled across so many channels and offices, and she found herself in yet another meeting with her supervisor.

She lifted her tired, dehydrated body out of her work chair and trudged down the hallway to her meeting. She had no energy to engage him verbally. She was always quick to say that in a battle of wits, he came unarmed. Today she didn't have the fight in her.

Jingles jingled his way into the room.

"Marsha, we had a clear understanding that you would no longer pursue the Philadelphia Police Department's murder investigation of the newspaper reporter. Given the amount of work our squad has and the tasks you were recently given to follow on the money trail of the Columbians, I cannot understand why you would interfere with a homicide investigation and take work time away from your appointed tasks."

"Have you received a complaint from the police department?" Marsha asked.

"They were concerned that the Bureau was running a separate and concurrent investigation into one of their cases where an arrest warrant had already been issued for the perpetrator."

"And how did you assuage their concerns, sir?"

"I told them that I will place you on written notice and that you are not to interfere further into their investigation. I told them you will immediately inform me of any future developments in that case before you take any action. Any. Action. And that you'll sign paperwork to that effect."

"I can see where your knowledge and expertise in these types of matters would aid the police department with the investigation," she replied.

Jingles' jowly flesh hanging around his neck and ears flushed red. He slid the letter across the desk for her signature receipt.

She signed it with a scrawl.

"Your personnel file is getting filled up with complaints and warnings, Agent O'Shea. This will not bode well for you when your performance evaluation is due."

"How can I argue with you, Supervisory Special Agent Stocker?"

She remained seated while Jingles jingled his way out of the small meeting room. She gazed out of the upper-level windows to the people scurrying about below.

She began asking herself, *Do I have "fuck me" tattooed on my forehead? Why is everybody telling me to stand down on this case? They don't know and can forever not know that if I had returned Menke's phone call, he might still be alive, and a lot of bloodshed might have been spared.* How long she sat there, she didn't know, until she saw Jingles making his way to the elevators. She glanced at her watch. 5:10pm. It was clockwork.

She hoisted herself from the swivel chair, much more tired and defeated than when she entered. *I'm done caring. Where is this getting me? Hollins has to run with it now. I can't do it anymore.*

Back at her desk, a FedEx envelope waited for her. She absent-mindedly opened it up and then saw a cover letter from the Temple University Bookstore. It read in part:

Dear Agent O'Shea.

The footage you requested from our store is enclosed. As you will see, a man paying with cash purchased a red Champion Hoodie, ball cap and red sweatpants during the late afternoon. The timestamps appear on the video. The clerk was careful to fold and box them for him. Good luck in your investigation.

The adrenaline surge was palpable. This time she got Ramit's attention gently, lest they have a repeat of pratfall from the day before.

"How are you doing, Ramit?"

"I am well, Marsha, how are you?"

"Couldn't be better. Seems I'm having trouble playing this on my tower. Can you give it a try?" The practiced nonchalance and even-breathing did not give away the internal swirl of emotions. Marsha, the gunslinger, was back.

Ramit took his usual care in loading the disc. When the video came up, he immediately saw the interior of a store.

"What are we looking for, Marsha?" he asked innocently enough.

"Guy in the red track suit that killed Stewart Menke, Ramit."

He craned his neck to look at her, and she placed a hand on his shoulder and nudged him to look at the screen.

In short order, a strong solidly-built white man, just under six foot appeared in front of the female cashier and handed over the goods. She lifted them up as if to show them off to the camera as she obsessively-compulsively folded the hoodie and pants before putting them in separate boxes. The cap was gently folded to go in the pants box. He handed her cash. She counted out change and gave him his change and his purchase. He smiled at her.

Ramit paused the disc at that point and made a screen capture and hit play again. The man walked away like a strutting pigeon.

Ramit silently took out the disc and then searched his hard-drive and brought up the surveillance picture of the man from the parking lot outside of the Old Man's wake. He put that picture next to the screenshot of the bookstore customer.

"Marsha, is that?" asked Ramit.

"That is Vladislav Balderis. Call Mike on your phone and put him on speaker," answered Marsha.

The speakerphone hissed, and she didn't give Mike a chance to say anything. "I found the guy with the red Temple tracksuit. It's the enforcer for the Russians. We saw his picture. He was the guy that stayed outside with all the other drivers and bodyguards at the Old Man's wake. His name is Vladislav Balderis."

Mike responded, "That son of a bitch."

"What?" Marsha asked.

"I can explain it later. Did you get a line on him?"

Now Ramit could jump in. "He has an electronics store on

Bustleton Avenue. And his listed residence for the business is . . . the Old Man's house."

"Great work, guys. Not to worry. I've got a way to find the bastard."

"Whaddaya mean I?" Marsha demanded.

"I thought your boss was putting you on the bench, Marsha," he said.

"Do I look like I'm on a bench?"

Mike didn't hesitate. "I'll pick you up."

She started to move into action but turned around to look at Ramit, who was giving her imploring eyes. "Ramit, I'm sorry. I need you to stay here and look after that disc. Too many people have already been hurt or had their lives screwed up, and I don't want that for you."

That hurt puppy look on his face was hard to miss and harder to ignore.

She added, "Our boss wants to hang me up by my thumbs or at least subject me to a thousand little paper cuts. I need you to carry on if anything happens to me. Protect the disc, don't let it out of the office. Let me take the fall for this if there's any problem. We solved a murder, Ramit."

With that, she gave him a crushing hug, before running back to her office for her purse and extra clips of ammo.

She looked at the letter from Jingles on her desk. She set her phone on it like a paperweight.

CHAPTER FORTY-EIGHT

"I've called around to all the area hospitals, and no one has a dead drunk matching the description of Sullivan," the source said.

"He told me that Sullivan drank himself to death," Vlad said.

"You know what Valnikov looks like. Was it the man in the delivery van at the courthouse?"

"I cannot say that it was not him. The photos you supplied are blurry and out of focus."

The source replied, "That was best we could do."

"How long have they been working together?" Vlad mused aloud.

"At least since Sullivan blew up his tent. Valnikov probably bought the fireworks."

Vlad reflexively rubbed his forearm. "Which wouldn't have happened if somebody had done their job right."

"Remind me again why we need to find a certain videotape from a strip club," came the source's quick retort.

Brushing that verbal slap aside, Vlad quickly realized how fortunate he was to have held the last meeting with the capos assembled at that location by Skype. "Valnikov hasn't been able to find me. He doesn't know my routines anymore."

"How can you be sure that he wants just to talk?" the source asked.

"I'm not waiting on him to tell me where and when he wants to kill me if that is what you are asking."

"What are your assets right now?" the source wondered.

"Right now, it's just the man in the car over there and me."

"Where?"

Blink your headlights, Vlad texted from his burner phone.

The headlights of a ratty, black ten-year-old Camry went on and off.

"Seems like you need some more help."

"I'm dealing with a weak old man and a drunk. They have been fortunate so far, and now they have just made it very easy for me."

The source shook his head. "It's your funeral."

"We took down the leadership of the Columbian cartels," Vlad said gesturing to the beat-up old car. "With one shot."

"Are you forgetting what it took to put you in the position to take that shot?" the source asked.

"No, I have not, my friend. What more are you hearing about the death of the reporter?" Vlad asked.

"Nothing since that FBI agent stuck her nose where it didn't belong," the source said.

"The car was in the garage that day, and she took her phone with her to the area of the liquor store. She then went with her workmate to a bar where they got drunk and sang terrible Karaoke songs." Vlad grimaced.

"What about now?" the source asked.

Vlad pulled out his clone phone from his satchel and replied, "Another late night at the office. What is this music called? She plays it all day long." The music came through the speaker.

"Country," the source said, recognizing Kenny knowing when to fold them.

CHAPTER FORTY-NINE

As Marsha and Mike drove to Valnikov's offices on the waterfront, he told her about his meetings with the Russian mobster.

Marsha chewed on her lip as they drove. "When did he come to you?"

"Over two weeks ago."

"After the fireworks display at F Troop?" she asked.

"Yep. Gotta think that he and Sullivan were connected at that point."

"Yeah, but Sullivan didn't come to me until two or three days later. I kinda got the sense that Sullivan didn't know he had the goods, only that some guy was coming after him, with that guy having killed his friend."

"So you're saying that they weren't sure it was Balderis who was good for the reporter, the accountant, and the mobster and dancer at the club," Mike said.

Marsha knew this patter. This was how investigators talked things out. Take this piece of the puzzle and added it to the other pieces, see how it fits. Try the piece in a different place, turn it around and try it somewhere else.

"The accountant got the video feed from the club, gave it to the reporter who sat on it too long and at the last minute handed it off to Sullivan."

"And Sullivan didn't know he had it until he sobered up and found it," Marsha added.

The pieces fit. "Gotta figure that Valnikov was the wheelman when Sullivan tried to turn himself in." Mike laid the next piece down.

"Only Balderis had me under surveillance since Stew's memorial service and cloned my phone. He knew that I was talking to Sullivan."

Mike nodded.

"Valnikov would know Balderis' crew and warned Sullivan at the last moment."

Their conversation ebbed as they pulled into the parking lot of Valnikov's front. The lights in the upstairs office turned off while they positioned the car to be able to watch the main entrance. An older woman exited the door and turned her back to them to lock the deadbolt. She turned and offered them a profile as she walked to the only car in the parking lot.

Mike reached for his door car handle, but Marsha placed her left hand on his right arm and held him back. "I've seen her before, gimme a second," she said.

Mike looked at her harder now and said, "Me too, but where?"

As the woman got closer to both of their cars, she fell under a bright flood light.

"She walked by me when I was on the sidewalk talking to Joe DiNatale after Stew's memorial service and—" Marsha said.

"And she was with a real religious Jew. All their men wear that same kind of black hat and have long curls," Mike finished.

"How'd you know?" Marsha asked.

"I saw them sitting in the parking lot of the accountant's wake where the Old Man was waked. You had the other side of the building remember?"

"The balls he had! He walked right by me with her," she said.

"Who?"

"Sullivan. Joseph Fucking Sullivan."

"He was the Jew? I would never have made him," he said.

"Nobody did. He must have gone to the memorial service with her and hid behind that disguise," Marsha countered.

"Follow her. Let's see where she leads us."

So they were tortured by this older woman who drove at or below the speed limit. She stopped at all of the stop signs and slowed down on yellow lights. She pulled into the driveway of a nondescript brick twin with a one car garage in Mayfair. The automatic garage door opened and closed behind her. Lights went on in the house, and she opened the front door and retrieved her mail from the mailbox next to the doorbell ringer. She closed the door and the timer lights for the driveway and porch extinguished. Mike ran the plates, and it came back to the woman of the house. "We can come back later if things don't pan out tonight."

They weren't far from the gentlemen's club. Happy hour was brisk, but the upstairs was dark. None of the cars in the parking lot raised an eyebrow for either of them. "We don't want to tip our hand just yet," he said staring at the biker dude at the front door.

"I don't know, Mike. I was kind of looking forward to getting a lap dance," Marsha deadpanned.

A few blocks over, they got out of his car and stretched their legs in a Bustleton Avenue strip mall shopping center.

"Wanna get a slice?" he asked.

They both grabbed a couple of extra cheese and pepperoni slices and a Coke.

Marsha said to the owner after he rung her up, "No wonder they didn't answer the phone over there. How am I supposed to return my flat screen? What happened?"

The pizzeria owner said, "You and a lotta of other people, middle of January it went up like a Roman candle. Nobody has been around since. Just the insurance adjustors. I'm lucky it didn't spread over here." He was talking about the electronics store owned by Vladislav Balderis that was burned out along with the nail salon on the other side and travel agency between on this side.

"Not even the owner?" Marsha asked between a sip and a bite.

"That cocky asshole? He's probably the one that torched the place, but you didn't hear that from me." The pizza guy started kneading some dough.

Marsha looked at Mike and nodded. They put down their slices and Cokes. With their hands freed, they both fished out their credentials and flashed them to the startled pizza-thrower.

"This him?" Mike handed him a picture of an Illinois driver's license and screenshot from the university bookstore video feed.

He dusted off his hands on his apron, took the photos to under a light and said, "Yep that's the asshole. Spoke with a Russian accent."

"How'd you know he was Russian?" It was Marsha's turn. The defective flat screen pretext, now forgotten.

"Lots of Russians up around here. You pick up on accents on the phone and then match the accent to the credit card when they come in for pick-up. We've got Cambodians, Brazilians, and all kinds, not like the old days when it was mostly Irish."

Mike asked, "What was the asshole's ride?"

"Oh yeah, he thought he was a big-shot gangster. He drove a black Chevy Suburban, all tinted-out like the Secret Service. It rode low. Wondered what he was always carrying in there."

Marsha thanked him with the ultimate compliment. "You throw a good pie, even better than the guys down in South Philly."

Then Mike added, "If you see the asshole or his ride, this is my personal number. It's always nice to have a get out of jail card from a police detective, don't you agree?"

The cynical store owner, who 20 minutes earlier wouldn't have given a snooping cop the time of day now almost swore an oath as they shook hands.

Back in the car. "The sauce came from a jar," Mike said.

"I didn't see you leave any crumbs," Marsha replied.

CHAPTER FIFTY

What was this Russian fixation with barnyard animals? Sully thought. They sat side by side in the solarium at the patio table staring into the pool. Inflatable pink pigs and yellow duckies floated lazily around. Arkady turned the water heater off but kept the water circulation pump on. The condensation on the windows cleared up, and Sully could see out into the moonless night. A quiet hum from the pump was the only sound in the glass enclosure.

"He will come." Arkady broke their silence.

"How many he will bring is the question," Sully replied.

Their common goal of ridding themselves of "Bad Vlad" had brought these two entirely different men closer together. Until a month ago, this crooked rich man now staring intently at the security monitors of his house and surrounding property would have little use for a piss-drunk street bum. But here they were, united in their need.

Wasn't it Arkady that warned me of Vlad's nighttime visit to F Troop? Didn't Arkady reluctantly drive me to the federal courthouse to turn myself in? Sully was not worried about Arkady's commitment to their mission.

Here it was playing out. Arkady was to be the goat with a bell around its neck tied to a post to be used as bait for the Siberian tiger. Did a friendship develop because of their enemy in common? Sully didn't think that he would be invited to Arkady's backyard barbecues when summer came around. That was the normal that Arkady needed; to go back to the way things were.

They both knew that sooner or later, Vlad would have made Arkady expendable. Arkady had poked the tiger one too many times. Russian goats and Siberian tigers didn't play well together, Sully concluded.

"He won't be alone that is for sure," Arkady said.

It was time for Sully to take up his position. They were betting on Vlad arriving under cover of darkness. There would be no negotiation. Men would die. It was Sully's job to make sure it wasn't Arkady.

Sully had already prepared his position in the grotto 100 yards away and had sighted in his hunting rifle there. With one more check of the comms and the camera feeds to his smartphone, he had ears and eyes on the inside of the solarium and would be able to execute his mission when he got the go-ahead from Arkady.

Sully rose to his feet. He was a warrior again. The exercise, rest, good food, shelter, no booze, and the right PTSD meds had quickly restored him physically to the professional killer from afar he once was. The focus and planning of this mission removed any doubt. He was a scary player in the drama about to unfold.

Arkady didn't bother to get up and said, "Kill him and all of his friends." He went back to scanning the monitors.

Sully exited the solarium through the back door of the pool house and walked behind dense evergreen trees to the tree line dividing Arkady's property from his neighbor's. He waited a few minutes until his eyes adjusted to the darkness. He moved from tree to tree looking all the time for any movement. It was slow going. He reached the spot where he would have to cross open ground to get to the grotto.

In the daytime, he had walked it. Tonight, he would crawl the same 50 yards on his belly. Crawling like this, he remembered slithering in the mud and cold rain of Parris Island and then the times across the hot sands or rough rock-strewn terrain of Afghanistan. On this ice-cold night under a starless sky, the frozen ground made the trek faster. He was almost to the grotto where his rifle and equipment were splayed out. With raw knees and elbows, he could have easily stood up and crouch-walked the last few yards of the ornamental planting surrounding the grotto.

A few more feet to go when he heard on his headset, "Hello, Arkady, I am surprised that you are not in bed at this hour." Worse, he heard it on the headset coming from a clump of bushes next to the grotto.

Marsha and Mike pulled down the curving driveway to Valnikov's mansion hidden from the road.

"Oh lookee, lookee," Marsha said as she nudged Mike. "What do we have here?"

They parked behind a black, tinted-out, riding-low-on-the-axles Chevy Suburban parked by the front door. They swept the interior with their flashlight, and then they laid their hands on the warm hood.

Marsha nodded and held her penlight in her right hand and with her automatic in her left hand. "I'll go around back and watch the rear."

Mike said, "No time for hero shit. We stick together and call from back-up."

Marsha was moving before he could argue and said, "Make

the call and then come around to the back. I'm not letting Menke's killer sneak out the back door."

Sully lurched to his feet from a prone position and threw a weak tackle on the scoped rifle and its holder pinning both to the ground. Sully's hands were on the rifle as the figure, a man dressed just like him, let go of the gun and pushed upward sending Sully and the gun in different directions.

Vlad and Arkady were standing now with the round patio table between them.

"Don't be stupid, Vlad, if anything happens to me the video gets sent to the Sicilians. There is nowhere you can hide from them." Arkady had the height advantage and looked down on the younger man. "I will call the shots from now on."

Vlad reached for the chair and sat down. "Arkady, I can be reasonable and listen to your proposal."

Arkady remained standing and repeated the code words to Sully. "You don't understand. I will call the shots from now on."

The dead silence lingered through the solarium as the two men stared at each other. Then across both of their comms came two words spoken from different voices.

"Sullivan."

"Asshole."

Arkady pulled out his pistol, as Vlad stood up doing the same.

"Freeze," yelled Marsha, as she entered the solarium from the pool house door.

The sniper unsheathed his combat knife. Sully did likewise with his Ka-Bar. They circled and lunged. Both righties had done this dance before. If Sully could get closer to his rifle, he might be able to get off a shot. The sniper faked a slide step and moved in on Sully, who barely sidestepped the thrust and locked the attacker's arm against his body with his right arm negating both the attack and his own defense.

~

"Put the guns down slowly and kick them away." Marsha crouched in her combat stance with a two-hand grip.

Neither man moved to lower their pistols as they stared at each other. "Two of you and one of me, who do I kill first?" Marsha said as she pointed her weapon at the midpoint between them.

"Correction, partner, two of us and two of them." Mike's voice came up from behind her. "Help is on the way. We can just sit tight. Now do what the lady says."

~

The sniper pulled on his own arm and yanked Sully backward into the grotto with a throw to the ground. Sully pulled just as hard on the sniper's arm, and they both slammed into the frozen ground.

~

Arkady looked past Hollins and watched a man stride from the darkness of the house into incandescent lighting of the solarium. "What's going on here?" he demanded. He held his gun in his left hand as he closed the distance to all the others in the tense stand-off.

Marsha turned and pointed her gun at the speaker. Recognition was immediate and confusing. "Nick!" Marsha yelled. "What the hell?"

"Trying to stay one step ahead of you so you wouldn't get killed. Now drop the guns, boys."

Both knives went flying into the bushes on impact. The younger and faster sniper got to his feet first and went right to Sully's throat with both hands. The sniper had Sully's legs pinned. Sully tried flailing with his arms to move the sniper from above him and to get him to release the death grip. Precious air was not finding Sully's searing lungs.

The sniper brought his face closer to Sully's. "Who is the asshole now," he hissed.

Blackness and stars replaced the leering killer's face. He tried one last time to pry loose the vice-like grip on his throat.

"Welcome to the party, Captain Drummond," Vlad said. "Better late than never."

Sully bucked his hips one last time and moved the stronger man just enough to get them closer to Sully's set up. Sully reached his hands out like he was making angels wings on the ground hoping for anything to use to break this stranglehold. He snagged his kit bag and his coffee thermos into hand's reach.

"Back up is on its way. We can sort this all out then," Hollins said.

Nick replied, "No, it's not. You are bluffing, Mike. I'm in charge now." He held out his portable radio. "All is quiet on the Western Front."

Sully was beginning to lose consciousness as he thumbed the lid off his coffee thermos and the steaming hot brew seared his hand. He turned his head and closed his eyes. He then whipped the sloshing burning liquid into the eyes of his assailant. The sniper reflexively reached for his burning face and eyes. With a whoosh of air, Sully inflated his chest bucking the man upwards. Sully head-butted the sniper's coffee-drenched face. The crack of the sniper's nose cartilage was immediately followed by the sniper's scream.

The sound of the scream wafted into the solarium.

"So much for your story about Mr. Sullivan drinking himself to death, Arkady," Vlad said.

"I wouldn't count him out yet, Vlad. How many times did you try to kill him?" Arkady countered.

Kneeling and breathing were good, Sully thought, but he had to move quickly to counter the sniper's blind charge. He reached for his hunting rifle and knew he couldn't turn it around in time and did the next best thing. He butt-stroked the sniper in the throat. The sniper grabbed the gun stock, but it slipped out of his coffee-soaked hands. He fell to his knees.

The pieces began to click in place. "That scumbag was always one step of me, Mike and now I know why," Marsha said.

"You couldn't leave it alone, Marsha, could you?", Nick yelled. "No matter what Dad or I said, you had to go sticking your nose where it don't belong."

"Drummond, how do you know this FBI agent?" Vlad asked.

Nick responded with a shot over Vlad's head. "I said I'm in charge here and nobody has to get hurt. Now drop your guns."

"Tell me what to do, Detective Hollins," Arkady said.

Marsha interrupted, "He's your source, Mike? Am I the only one being played here?"

Just like tee-ball when I was a kid, Sully thought, as he gripped the cold steel of the rifle's barrel like the varsity baseball player he had been twenty years earlier. Keep your eye on the ball.

Hands, wrist, arms, shoulders, torso and hips moved in perfect oneness—the polished walnut stock connected with a sickening *thwapp* to the right side of the sniper's head. The crushed skull pulled the rest of the body with a sickening lifeless thud on the ground several feet away.

Sully sat down with the broken rifle in his hands. It had snapped at the trigger guard. His breathing did not return to normal. It became more ragged with anxiety. No! No! Blackness was closing in.

"No, Marsha, you are not the only one being played here. Arkady, you too, drop it," Mike said.

Both Russians slowly dropped their guns on the floor. "Now kick them away," Nick said.

Vlad realized that he had to make a move as his gun slid away on the slick pool deck and spoke quickly. "So this is how you treat your employer, someone you have killed for, Captain Drummond."

"Shut up the fuck up, Vlad," Nick said.

"That's right. This man works for me." Leering at Nick, he continued. "Tell them why you have so much to lose if we don't find the thumb drive. It has more on it than just the gentlemen's club video."

"The next one is in your head, Vlad," Nick replied.

Hollins was staring at Nick and was next to chime in. "Keep talkin', Vlad. I am curious to hear what you have to say about my brother in blue."

"First tell me how Drummond knows Agent O'Shea."

"He's my brother, dipshit. Of course, you would have learned that from watching the news after ambushing me and Sullivan at the courthouse. Now answer the man's question." Marsha's gaze shifted to her brother as well.

Vlad, seeing his success in playing the people with the guns against each other, poured gasoline on the fire. "The accountant gave the reporter records on thirty years of bribes to the police department."

"Sis, do you see why I wanted you so far away from this thing? It's much bigger than you think. The false flags, the subway, and train bombings, it was all meant to take you away from this insanity. We can still fix this."

"So you're the fuckin' rat." Hollins shifted his pistol towards Nick.

Marsha was torn between her love for her brother and her duty and honor. "You're wrong, Nicky."

Vlad slowly reached for his ankle holster.

Semper Fi, Stew, Semper Fi. Semper Fi, Stew, Semper Fi, Sully kept repeating the mantra until the blackness receded and his breathing returned to adrenaline-dumping post fight-to-the-death normal. His attention focused on the crumpled man at his feet. He toed the body over onto its back. The sneering son of a bitch now had a lopsided slack-jawed look of a rotting jack o'lantern. That man was sent to kill him and Arkady. Arkady, Oh God, the Mission. He reached for where his headset was. It got knocked off in the fight.

Retracing his steps to the bushes around the grotto, he picked up the sniper's headset and heard the angry voices of the cops arguing and echoing, but could hear a Russian speaking clearly. There was no mistaking that voice. It was the same one he heard right after the fireworks at F Troop.

His gun was worthless. He began running his hand through the bushes. There was no mistaking the cold metal of a barrel, and he lifted a foreign bolt-action rifle with a scope. He chambered a round, returned to his position and set out the bi-pod and brought his eye to the scope.

Marsha watched in horror as Nick swung on Hollins and fired. Vlad reached for his snub-nose and sent a round toward Nick. Arkady tackled Vlad from behind. Marsha was torn between caring for Hollins or her brother. Both lay bleeding on opposite sides of the pool.

Hollins rasped, "Don't let them get away." Blood was saturating his dress shirt from the hole next to the rider on the polo pony. She unwound her scarf and bunched it up over the hole and took both of his hands and placed them on top. The weight of his meaty hands was enough to stem the bleeding.

"Don't go anywhere, partner, I'll be right back."

He offered a weak smile and stifled a bloody cough.

She raised to see Vlad lifting Arkady to his feet and using him as a shield. She drew on him, but Arkady's girth prevented a clean shot.

"Drop your gun, Agent O'Shea or I kill him."

"No dice, Vlad. Kill him, and I drop you like a sack of potatoes. It's over, Vlad. Give it up."

"I am not sure why my man in the woods hasn't killed you yet, Agent O'Shea." With the revolver pressed against Arkady's temple, Vlad pulled Arkady backward toward the sliders from the pool into the darkened house.

Sully had watched through the scope how the bodies dropped like dominoes, hearing the gunshots first through the headset and then as muffled pops from behind the glass.

He had to take the shot. Arkady would be dead before they reached the other end of the solarium. Vlad kept his hostage close.

"No more, Vlad. It's over." Nick, holding his guts in with one hand, raised his gun toward the retreating Russians.

As Vlad took his gun off of Arkady's temple to point it at Nick, Arkady bent at the waist and yelled, "SULLIVAN!"

Sully had the crosshairs of a scope that had been zeroed in for another shooter on Vlad's upper torso and squeezed off a round from a gun that he never fired before.

Vlad's shot went high as he was spun sideways from the high-powered slug tearing into his gun hand shoulder. With his right leg, Vlad sent Arkady stumbling towards Marsha. Sully heard more gunfire before the wounded Siberian tiger disappeared through the sliders.

Sully began running to the solarium. He saw Arkady get to his feet with a handgun. Marsha ran to her brother.

Arkady's tracksuit was a bloody mess from the theatrical blood sheet covering the body armor. He and Sully stared at the bullet lodged in the vest in the middle of his back.

"Did you get him?" Arkady asked.

"No, he disappeared into the dark. He's a wounded and dangerous animal," Sully said.

"He's done here in America. He is no longer a threat to us," Arkady replied.

They went around the pool to Marsha's partner.

Arkady said, "Detective Hollins. We will get you help." Sully was already pulling out medical supplies and began dressing the wound.

"Marsha, why couldn't you let it go? Look at this mess."

Marsha was cradling her dying brother in her arms. She rocked him in her lap. She was crying. "Oh, Nicky, I am so sorry. I am so sorry. Don't die on me."

"Promise me it stops here, Marsha, tell me you are done with it. Promise me." He reached up to touch her lips. "No more."

Sully finished dressing Hollins chest wound. Arkady had called for help.

They began quick timing it to Marsha kneeling over her

brother doing chest compressions. Sully was leading Arkady when the solarium exploded in shattering glass as the black, heavily-tinted Chevy Suburban crashed through, hitting Arkady straight on.

Sully's reaction time saved him from the direct impact, but a crumpled aluminum girder got snagged on the twisted bumper and hooked him into the water. The quickly submerging land barge brought him down below the surface as the driver's side door opened. Sully wriggled himself out of the winter camouflage coat as his air was giving out. He was free and started to kick to the surface and that big gulp of sweet fresh air when he was dragged downward.

Vlad was pulling down on Sully's left leg with his good arm. Vlad had a death grip on him. Sully tried thrashing and kicking with his other leg. He was sinking lower and lower, and the light from above was getting dimmer. As his breath ended, he used his remaining strength to reach into his pant's cargo pocket and pulled out the multi-purpose tool, plunging its four-inch blade into Vlad's neck again and again. Blood red water gave way to blackness.

He coughed violently. Water gushed from his lungs, and he breathed in, coughed out water from his nose and mouth again. He sucked in more air and opened his eyes to see Marsha's face hovering above his. Her hair was soaking wet and dripping on him. Her clothes looked like she took a shower in them. Slowly the coughing and gagging subsided. He could feel his fingers and toes. He moved his arms and legs. *So far. So good. Nothing hurt and everything worked.*

"Marsha." He coughed again and laid his head back down.

"Sully," she replied with the slightest worried smile.

"Is he dead?"

"Yeah."

"Arkady?"

"Him too."

"Nicky?"

"Yeah."

"I don't know where Arkady kept his, but here's mine." He slipped her the thumb drive.

She took it and said, "A lot of people died for this stupid thing." She slipped it into her coat pocket.

"I didn't kill Stew. I'm sorry about your brother, but what else could I do?" He looked into her eyes as they heard the sound of sirens approaching.

She stifled back her tears, sniffled back a running nose, looked away, and then back at him. "He almost killed a good, honest cop. He was dirty. I shoulda known by the way he was warning me off this case." She pulled him to a seated position and patted him on the back.

He was returning the pats when the Lower Merion police officers burst into the carnage of what was once the happy place of one of their wealthier homeowners.

CHAPTER FIFTY-ONE

Ballistics matched the stories of Marsha and Sully exactly. Both of their stories, given separately, over several sessions, matched with only minor differences.

Marsha's statement included Vlad admitting to killing both the accountant and Stew Menke. The fibers from the cargo deck of the Suburban, fished out of the pool, matched the carpet fibers stuck to the plastic wrapping around the rug the accountant was sent down the river in. Sully's statement about the college kid in the tracksuit and the videotape from the university bookstore further corroborated Vlad's admission. Sully's alibi was solid with the liquor store tape.

The fallout from the Lower Merion shoot-out was still ongoing. Three dead Russian gangsters, one wounded and one dead Philadelphia cop along with a bribery scandal going back decades.

Gigi Falcone was released from prison and filed a multi-million-dollar civil suit, but his set-up by the Mad Russian would be difficult to extend to the cops who were not admitting that they had gotten the anonymous tip to stop his car.

The Dagestanis were likewise vindicated when a search

warrant of Nick Drummond's apartment uncovered evidence of their frame-up. They decided to go back to Dagestan rather than endure years of wrangling to get their fair compensation.

It was discovered that the unassuming mob boss had tentacles deep and wide into the city's and state's many bureaucracies.

The remaining Russian capos circled the wagons, making it clear to the other groups that Vlad went rogue, which was made evident by his killing of three of their own. They quickly cut a deal with the Sicilian to reverse the protection and payments.

Marsha was placed on administrative leave. A dead cop and disobeying a direct written order with the ink still wet was pretty self-explanatory. She maintained that she was invited by the Philadelphia Police Department and her Federal jurisdiction allowed them to cross City Line Avenue into Montgomery County. She pointed out that her boss had clocked out before her that night. He never made provisions for his squad to reach him at night and that the exigent circumstances called for immediate action.

She and Hollins did prevent the first attempt on Valnikov's life and were eventually successful in solving the case of Menke's death as being mob-related. Hollins was recovering but had suffered a partial loss of use of his left arm.

"What are you going to do, Marsha?" Ramit asked.

They were sitting at their new favorite Country-Western bar in the back corner, away from the Karaoke machine and the two-step dance floor, where the urban cowboys twirled their urban cowgirls. It had been snowing all day with a good Nor'easter pummeling the Delaware Valley.

"Dunno, no plans, can't even go to my own brother's funeral. All those blue suits and my Mom and Dad sitting there. Would be really uncomfortable."

Ramit looked at the shot glasses that outnumbered the beer bottles in front of her. "I'm worried about you, Marsha."

"Ramit, I am worried about me too. Seems like I have a knack for putting people in harm's way."

During Happy Hour, she had filled him in on the courthouse bomb threat.

She turned over a shot glass. "First it was Menke, for not listening to a freaking phone call, a freaking phone call."

Ramit tapped the bottom of the upturned glass. "Have you maybe thought about traveling? Taking a vacation? Going some-where quiet?"

She slammed another shot glass over. "Then there was Sullivan and all the people at the courthouse, innocent fucking people." A couple more shot glasses tapped loudly down on the wooden surface.

The fifth shot glass pounded the table. "Then there was Mike Hollins. I almost got him killed, Ramit. I almost got him killed."

The bouncer in his tight black T-shirt, earbud and bulging biceps made his way to their table.

"Is there a problem here, ma'am? You're getting a little loud," the bouncer asked.

She looked up and focused on him. "Yes, there is. I am kryp-tonite. People around me die, and don't call me ma'am."

Ramit took her by the arm and said, "We are leaving now, sir."

"Whaddabout my older brother, Nicky? Whaddabout Nicky?" Masha pulled her arm away from Ramit, gave the bouncer a don't-you-dare-touch-me look. She got up on her own two unsteady feet.

"We're leaving," she slurred.

Marsha stumbled to the door with Ramit clearing the way.

～

About the same time, in a Cape Cod up in Bucks County on a snow-covered street where the wind buffeted the house and whistled through its old wooden windows, a little girl snuggled in her bed between her two parents. "Read me that story again, Daddy."

So Sully did.

The End

Want more Marsha? Want to find out what happens next Click here for Clearwater Blues Book 2 in the Marsha O'Shea Series.
Clearwater Blues

HERE IS MY ASK

Reviews are the life blood of Independent Authors
If you liked this book, please leave a review with the retailer where you made your purchase. It's the best way to help other readers discover a page turner that they will enjoy too.

ALSO BY JOHN A HODA

Second Chance at Bat

Joe DiNatale is a 39-year-old insurance salesman and little league coach who discovers he has a magical pitch. He gets a one-in-a-million shot to try out for his beloved Philadelphia Phillies. Follow this "Average Joe" on a roller coaster ride from the small town life to instant stardom.

Second Chance at Bat

MUGSHOT: MY FAVORITE DETECTIVE STORIES

Come ride around the country with veteran investigator John A. Hoda as he searches for the truth. He has selected great stories from his four decade career and keeps serving them up like free refills of coffee at the twenty-four hour diner.

Mugshots: My Favorite Detective Stories

Become an email subscriber for upcoming announcements, bonus gifts, cover reveals and discounts
https://johnhodaauthor.mailerpage.com/contact

ACKNOWLEDGMENTS

I would like to give a big thank you to John Adamus, my editor for challenging me to write a better story. I am grateful to Margaret Zeiders for her sharp red pencil on the line edits. Thanks to my beta readers Marc Sirkin, Lisa Garcia. Skip Zeiders and Robin Vierow for reminding me that a good story needs good storytelling to become a bonafide page-turner.

Diane Cowan and Kitty Hailey, Philly Private Investigators and mentors who both told me who to talk to and where to turn for my research.

Marine Neal Conlon for his real-life insights into the sandbox of Afghanistan.

Salvador Fede, one of Philadelphia's Finest who helped me with Police Department's Org Chart and procedure.

Mike Clark and Kenneth Gray, former FBI agents and now professors at the University of New Haven who both patiently answered my questions about the inner-workings of the Bureau.

Finally, thank you Dominic Forbes for designing a badass book cover.

DEDICATION

For Gloria, Emily, and John Michael, my loving family. Thank you so much for supporting and encouraging me.

ABOUT THE AUTHOR

John A. Hoda is an award-winning author (The Legal Investigator) and headline-making investigator He graduated in 1975 with a B.S. in Criminology from Indiana University of Pennsylvania. He is a former police officer, insurance fraud investigator and for the last 29 years has run a successful PI business. He has written numerous articles for *PI Magazine* and has created the DVD: *The Ultimate Guide to Taking Statements*. He has sat on the boards of both the National Association of Legal Investigators and The Connecticut Association of Licensed Private Investigators. He is a Certified Legal Investigator and a Certified Fraud Examiner.

Want more detective stories? Come visit John at the All Things Investigative website at https://johnhodaauthor.mailerpage.com/contact

Police Cadet Ashley Jansen told a lie when she was eight years old and telling the truth now may get her kicked off the force or killed.

Moral courage and truth in policing in this post-truth world is more important than ever. Sign up for my newsletter and I will keep you abreast of all the developments and some surprises.

COPYRIGHT PAGE

Copyright Page

John A. Hoda © 2019.

www.ingramcontent.com/pod-product-compliance
Lightning Source LLC
Chambersburg PA
CBHW061027120726
47910CB00006B/2130